Juan Rulfo was born in Sayula, in the state of Jalisco, Mexico, in 1918. He studied at the universities of Guadalajara and Mexico City, and was twice a fellow at the Centro Mexicano de Escritores. His first book, published in 1953, was a collection of short stories entitled *El Llano En Llamas* (*The Valley in Flames*). *Pedro Páramo* is his first novel.

PEDRO PÁRAMO

by

Juan Rulfo

Translated by Lysander Kemp

GROVE PRESS, INC.   NEW YORK

I came to Comala because I was told that my father, a certain Pedro Páramo, was living here. My mother told me so, and I promised her I would come to see him as soon as she died. I pressed her hand so that she'd know I would do it, but she was dying and I was in the mood to promise her anything. "Be sure you go and visit him," she told me. "I know he'll be pleased to see you." So all I could do was to keep telling her I would do it, and I kept on saying it until I had to pry my hand loose from her dead fingers.

Before that she told me, "Don't ask him for anything that isn't ours. Just for what he should have given me and didn't. Make him pay for the way he forgot us."

"All right, Mother."

I didn't intend to keep my promise. But then I began to think about what she told me, until I couldn't stop thinking and even dreaming about it, and building a whole world around that Pedro Páramo. That's why I came to Comala.

It was in the dog-days, when the hot August wind is poisoned by the rotten smell of the saponaria, and the road went up and down, up and down. They say a road goes up or down depending on whether you're coming or going. If you're going away it's uphill, but it's downhill if you're coming back.

"What's the name of that village down there?"

"Comala, señor."

"You're sure it's Comala?"

"Yes, señor."

"Why does it look so dead?"

"They've had bad times, señor."

I expected it to look the way it did in my mother's memories. She was always sighing for Comala, she was homesick and wanted to come back, but she never did. Now I was coming back in her place, and I remembered what she told me: "There's a beautiful view when you get to Los Colimotes. You'll see a green plain . . . it's yellow when the corn is ripe. You can see Comala from there. The houses are all white, and at night it's all lighted up." Her voice was soft and secret, almost a whisper, as if she were talking to herself.

"And why are you going to Comala?" I heard him ask me.

"To see my father."

"Oh," he said.

And we were silent again.

We were walking downhill, hearing the steady trot of the burros. Our eyes were half-closed, we were so tired and sleepy in the August heat.

"They'll give you a fine party," he said. "They'll be glad to see somebody again. It's been years since anybody came here."

Then he added: "It's you, so they'll be glad to see you."

The heat shimmered on the plain like a transparent lake. There was a line of mountains beyond the plain, and beyond that, nothing but the distance.

"What does your father look like?"

"I don't know," I said. "I just know that he's called Pedro Páramo."

"Oh."

But the way he said it, it was almost like a gasp. I said, "At least that's what they told me his name was."

I heard him say, "Oh," again.

I met him in Los Encuentros, where three or four roads come together. I was just waiting there, and finally he came by with his burros.

"Where are you going?" I asked him.

"That way, señor," he said, pointing.

"Do you know where Comala is?"

"That's where I'm going."

So I followed him. I walked along behind, keeping up with his steps, until he understood I was following him and slowed down a little. After that we walked side by side, almost touching shoulders.

He said, "Pedro Páramo is my father too."

A flock of crows flew across the empty sky, crying *caw, caw, caw.*

After we crossed the ridge we started downhill again. We left the warm air up there and walked down into pure heat without a breath of air in it. Everything looked as if it were waiting for something.

"It's hot here," I said.

"This is nothing. Just wait, you'll be a lot hotter when you get to Comala. That town's the hottest place in the world. They say that when somebody dies in Comala, after he arrives in Hell he goes back to get his blanket."

"Do you know Pedro Páramo?" I asked him.

I dared to ask him questions because I had an idea I could trust him.

"Who is he?" I asked.

"He's hate. He's just pure hate."

He lashed the burros even though he didn't need to, because they were keeping ahead of us down the slope.

I had my mother's picture in my shirt pocket and I could feel it warming my heart, as if she were sweating too. It was an old picture, all frayed at the edges, but it was the only one I knew about. I found it in the kitchen in a box full of herbs, and I've kept it ever since. My mother hated to have her picture taken. She said pictures were for witchcraft, and maybe she was right, because the picture was full of holes, like needle holes. Near the heart there was a hole so big you could put your middle finger into it.

It's the same picture I have with me now. I hope it'll help me with Pedro Páramo when he recognizes who it is.

"Look," he said, stopping. "See that mountain, the one that looks like a pig's bladder? Good. Now look over there. See the ridge of that mountain? Now look over here. See that mountain way off there? Well, all that's the Media Luna, everything you can see. And it all belongs to Pedro Páramo. He's our father, but we were born on a petate on the floor. And the real joke is that he took every one of us to be baptized. He took you, didn't he?"

"I don't know."

"You go to hell."

"What did you say?"

"I said we're almost there, señor."

"I know. But what about the village? It looks deserted."

"That isn't how it looks. It is. Nobody lives there any more."

"And Pedro Páramo?"

"Pedro Páramo died a long time ago."

It was the hour when the children play in the streets in every village, filling the afternoon with their shouts. When the walls still reflect the yellow light of the sun.

At least that's what I saw in Sayula yesterday at the same hour. I also saw the doves flying in the still air. They circled around and disappeared over the rooftops, and the shouts of the children flew up like birds.

Now I was here in this silent village. I heard the sound of my footsteps on the fieldstones that paved the streets. A hollow sound, echoing against the walls.

I was walking down the main street, past the empty houses with their broken doors and their weeds. What did what's-his-name call that weed? "Captain's wife, señor. It's a pest that just waits till a house is empty, then it moves in. You'll see what it's like."

When I was passing a corner I saw a woman wrapped up in a rebozo, but she disappeared as if she didn't even exist. I kept on walking, looking into the open doorways. Suddenly she crossed the street in front of me.

"Good evening," she said.

I followed her with my eyes. "Where does Doña Eduviges live?" I called to her.

And she pointed: "There. The house next to the bridge."

I knew that her voice was a living human voice. That she had teeth in her mouth, and a tongue that moved when she talked, and eyes like the eyes of everybody else on earth.

It was growing dark.

She called out, "Good night!" to me. There weren't any children playing, or any doves, but I felt that the village was still alive, and that if I didn't hear anything except the silence, that was because I wasn't used to silence, with my head still so full of noises and voices.

Especially voices. And here where the air was so dead, they sounded even louder. I remembered what my mother told me: "You'll hear me better there, better than now. I'll be nearer to you there." My mother . . . living.

I'd wanted to tell her, "You made a mistake, you didn't give me the right directions. You told me where this was and that was, and here I am in a dead village, looking for somebody who doesn't even exist."

I found the house at the bridge by walking toward the sound of the river, and knocked on the door. Or I tried to. But my hand just knocked on empty air, as if the wind had opened the door. A woman stood there. She said: "Come in."

And I went in.

I stayed in Comala. Before he left me, the man with the burros said: "I'm going farther on. My house is over there, where the mountains come together. If you want to come along, you'll be welcome. But if you want to stay here, go ahead, even if it's just to take a look at the village. Maybe you'll find somebody living."

I stayed. That's what I came to do.

"Where can I find a place to stay?" I called to him. I almost had to shout.

"Look for Doña Eduviges, if she's still alive. Tell her I sent you."

"What's your name?"

"Abundio . . ." But I couldn't hear his last name.

"I'm Eduviges Dyada. Come in."

It looked as if she'd been waiting for me. She said everything was ready, and I followed her through a long row of dark rooms. They seemed empty at first, but when I got used to the darkness and the narrow thread of light that followed us, I could see shadows on both sides. I thought we must be walking through a passageway between piles of bundles.

"What have you got in here?" I asked.

"Junk," she said. "The whole house is full of junk. All those that went away picked this house to keep their furniture and belongings in, and they don't come back for them. But the room I've kept for you is at the rear. I always keep the junk out of it, in case somebody comes back. And so you're her son, then?"

"Whose?"

"Doloritas's."

"Yes . . . but how do you know?"

"She told me you were coming. She said you'd arrive today."

"Who? My mother?"

"Yes."

I didn't know what to think, and she didn't explain.

"This is your room," she said.

There wasn't any door, just an opening, and when she lit the candle I could see it was empty.

"It doesn't have any bed," I told her.

"Don't worry about that. You're tired, and just being tired is enough of a mattress. You can sleep on the floor, and I'll fix your bed tomorrow. You ought to know it isn't easy to furnish a room on the spur of the moment. You have to know in advance, and your mother didn't let me know till just today."

"My mother . . . my mother is dead."

"Oh, then that's why her voice sounded so weak. As if she were a long way away. Now I understand. And when did she die?"

"Seven days ago."

"Poor Dolores. She must have felt deserted. We promised each other we'd die together. So that we could give each other courage on the way, in case it was necessary. In case there were any difficulties. We were very close friends. Didn't she ever talk to you about me?"

"No, never."

"That's strange. We made that promise when we were girls. And it was just after she was married. But we were very fond of each other. Your mother was so pretty, so . . . well, let's say so sweet, you couldn't help loving her. But I'm sure I'll catch up with her. I know how far away Heaven is, all right, but I know the shortcuts. You just die, God willing, when you want to, not when He arranges it. Or if you want you can make Him arrange it earlier. Excuse me for talking to you like this, but I can't help thinking of you as my son. Yes, I've said many times, 'Dolores's son should have been mine.' I'll tell you why later. The only thing I want to tell you right now is that I'll catch up with her on one of the roads to Heaven."

I thought the woman must be crazy. Then I didn't think anything at all, except that I must be in some other world. My body seemed to be floating, it was so limp, and you could have played with it as if it were a rag doll.

"I'm tired," I said.

"First come and eat something. A little something or other."

"I will. But later."

The water that dripped from the roof-tiles was making a hole in the sand in the patio. It fell drip, drip, drip on a laurel leaf, and the leaf bowed down and bobbed up again. The storm had already passed. Now and then, when the wind shook the branches of the pomegranate tree, there was a little shower under the tree, printing the ground with brilliant drops for a moment until they sank in and blurred. During the storm the chickens were all hunched up as if asleep, but now they stretched their wings and strutted out into the patio, gobbling up the earthworms the rain brought out. The sun glowed on the stones, lit everything up with colors, drank up the water from the earth, played with the shining air that played with the leaves.

"What are you doing in the toilet so long?"

"Nothing, Mamá."

"If you stay there, a snake'll come and bite you."

"Yes, Mamá."

I was thinking of you, Susana. In the green hills. When we flew kites in the windy season. We heard the sounds of the village down below us while we were up there, up on the hill, and the wind was tugging the string away from me. 'Help me, Susana.' And gentle hands grasped my hands. 'Let out more string.'

The wind made us laugh; our glances met while the string paid out between our fingers; but it broke, softly, as if it had been struck by the wings of a bird. And up there the paper bird fell in somersaults, dragging its rag tail, until it was lost in the green of the earth.

Your lips were moist, as if they had been kissing the dew.

"I told you to come out of the toilet."

"Yes, Mamá. Right away."

I was remembering you. When you were there looking at me with your sea-green eyes.

He looked up and saw his mother in the doorway.

"Why are you taking so long? What are you doing?"

"I'm thinking."

"Can't you think somewhere else? It isn't good for you to spend so much time in the toilet. Besides, you ought to be working at something. Why don't you go to your grandmother's to help with the corn?"

"All right, Mamá. Right away."

"Grandmother, I'm going to help with the corn."

"We've already finished . . . but we're going to make some chocolate. Where have you been? We were looking for you all during the storm."

"I was in the other patio."

"What were you doing? Praying?"

"No, Grandmother. I was just watching it rain."

His grandmother looked at him with those eyes of hers, half-yellow and half-gray, that seemed to look inside a person and read his thoughts.

"Well, then, go and clean the mill."

Susana, you are miles and miles away, above all the clouds, far away above everything, hidden. Hidden in His immensity, behind His Divine Providence, where I can never find you or see you. Where my words can never reach you.

"Grandmother, the mill's broken."

"That Micaela must have broken it. She breaks everything in the house, and she just won't learn. But there's no help for it."

"Why don't we buy a new one? This one's so old it isn't worth fixing."

"I suppose you're right. But it cost so much to bury your grandfather, and then all these tithes to the church, I don't think there's a centavo in the house. Well, we'll simply have to sacrifice ourselves and buy a new one. Go see Doña Inés Villalpando and ask her to give us one on credit until October. We can pay her out of the harvest."

"Yes, Grandmother."

"And while you're at it, tell her to lend us a sifter and a pruning-knife. The way all these plants are growing, pretty soon they'll crowd us out into the street. If I still had my big house with the land out back and all, I wouldn't complain, but your grandfather sold it when we came here. God knows nothing ever comes out the way you want it to. Tell Doña Inés that we'll pay her what we owe her out of the harvest."

"Yes, Grandmother."

There were hummingbirds in the patio. It was that time of year. They were buzzing among the jasmine flowers.

He went past the doorway of the Sacred Heart and found twenty-four centavos. He left four centavos and kept the twenty.

Before he left, his mother asked him: "Where are you going?"

"To Doña Inés Villalpando's, to buy a new mill. The old one's broken."

"Tell her to give you a yard of black taffeta and put it on our bill."

"All right, Mamá."

"And on your way back, buy me some aspirins. There's some money in the flowerpot in the entry."

He found a peso. He left his twenty centavos and took the peso.

"Now," he thought, "I've got more than enough money, no matter what happens."

"Pedro!" they shouted at him, "Pedro!"

But he didn't hear them. He was far away.

It rained again in the night. He listened to the drumming of the water for a long while, but then he fell asleep, and when he woke up all he could hear was a quiet drizzle. The windowpane was glazed with water, and the heavy drops ran down it like tears. *I was watching the drops fall, Susana, in the glare of the lightning, and every breath I breathed was a sigh, and every thought was a thought of you.*

The rain turned into a breeze. He heard: "The forgiveness of our sins and the resurrection of the flesh. Amen." That was inside, where the women were finishing the Rosary. They stood up, bolted the door, and put out the light.

All that was left was the night-light, and the sound of the rain, like the chirping of crickets . . .

"Why didn't you come to the Rosary? You know we're still praying for your grandfather."

His mother stood there in the shadow of the doorway, with a candle in her hand. Her shadow quivered on the ceiling. It was long and spread out, and the beams broke it up into pieces.

He said: "I don't feel well."

She went away. She put out the candle. When she closed the door and went away, the sobs came, mingled with the sob of the rain.

The church clock rang the hours, one after another, one after another, as if somehow time had shriveled.

"As I said, I almost was your mother. Didn't she tell you about it?"

"No. She never told me anything like that. I heard about you from somebody named Abundio. I didn't catch his last name, but he drives burros."

"Of course, Abundio. So he still remembers me! I used to give him a tip for every person he brought to the house. But everything's different now, with the village so poor, and nobody ever comes here. You say he recommended me to you?"

"He told me to be sure to look for you."

"I can't help being grateful to him. He was a good man, Abundio. Dependable, you know. He used to carry the mail, even after he went deaf. I remember the day it happened. We all felt sorry for him, because we liked him, he used to carry the mail and tell us what was happening out there in the world. I expect he told them out there what was going on back here. He was a great one to talk. And then he stopped talking, just like that. He said it wasn't any use talking if you couldn't hear what you were saying. What happened was that one of those sky-rockets, the kind that explodes, went off right over his head. After that he didn't talk, even though he still could. But he was a good man, Abundio, even so."

"The man I told you about wasn't deaf."

"No? Then it couldn't be the same one. Besides, Abundio's dead. I'm sure he must be dead. Didn't he tell you? It couldn't be the same one."

She shook her head.

"But to get back to your mother," she said. "I was going to tell you . . ."

I listened, but I also looked at her closely. I thought she must have suffered a lot at some time in her life. Her face was so pale, you would think there wasn't any blood in her body, and her hands were all wrinkled and withered up. You couldn't see her eyes. She had on an old white dress with a lot of lace, and a medal of the Virgin on a piece of twine, with the words *Refuge of Sinners.*

". . . And as I was saying, he was the man who tamed horses in the Media Luna. His name was Inocencio Osorio but everybody called him The Jumpingjack because he was so light on his feet. Pedro said he was good at breaking in colts, but he was good at something else, too, and it wasn't taming, it was stirring things up. I mean at stirring up dreams, and that's the truth. He had an affair with your mother, and with lots of others. Including myself. One time when I was sick he came to the

house and said, 'I'm going to examine you, so you'll get better.'
When he said that it always meant he'd handle you all over,
first just your fingertips, then rubbing your hands, then your
arms, until finally he got to your legs, rubbing and rubbing, so
that if they were cold before, pretty soon they were hot. And
all the time he'd be telling you your fortune. He'd go into a
sort of trance and roll his eyes like a gypsy, and sometimes he'd
end up stark naked because he said that's what we wanted.
Sometimes he'd be right, too. He couldn't be wrong every time.

"But what I wanted to tell you is that when this Osorio went
to see your mother he told her she shouldn't have anything to
do with any man that night, because the moon was very un-
favorable.

"So Dolores came to tell me she didn't know what to do. She
said she couldn't go to bed with Pedro Páramo, even though it
was their wedding night. I tried to tell her not to pay any attention to Osorio, he was nothing but a liar and a swindler.

"'I can't do it,' she said. 'You go in my place. He'll never know
the difference.'

"Of course I was a lot younger than she was, and not quite so
dark-skinned, but he wouldn't be able to tell in the darkness.

"'I can't do it, Dolores. You've got to sleep with him yourself.'

"'Please do me this one favor. I'll pay you back with others.'

"In those days your mother was a girl with meek eyes. If there
was anything really beautiful about her, it was her eyes. And
she knew how to talk you into anything.

"'Please go in my place,' she said.

"And I went.

"The darkness helped me, and so did something she didn't
know, which was that I liked Pedro Páramo too.

"I got into bed with him, full of love, and embraced him, but he'd been out on a spree the day before and was all tired out. He coughed and coughed but all he did was put his legs between mine.

"I got up before dawn and went to see Dolores. I said:

" 'Now you go. It's another day.'

" 'What did he do with you?' she asked.

" 'I don't know yet,' I said.

"You were born the next year. I wasn't your mother, but I almost was.

"I suppose your mother was embarrassed to tell you about all this."

My mother. ". . . *Green fields. You can see the horizon rise and fall when the wind moves in the wheat, or when the rain ruffles it in the afternoon. The color of the earth, the smell of alfalfa and bread. A village that smells of new honey . . .*"

"She always hated Pedro Páramo. 'Doloritas! Have you told them to fix my breakfast?' And your mother would get up before dawn to light the fire. The cats would wake up and follow her around, a whole parade of them. 'Doña Doloritas!'

"How many times did your mother hear that? 'Doña Doloritas, I can't eat this, it's cold.' How many times? And even though she was used to the worst, those meek eyes of hers began to harden."

". . . *And everything had the flavor of orange-blossoms in the warmth of the season . . .*"

"Finally she began to sigh.

" 'Why are you sighing, Doloritas?'

"I was with them that afternoon. We were out in the fields watching the flocks of little birds, and there was one buzzard circling in the sky.

"'Why are you sighing, Doloritas?'

"'I'd like to be a buzzard like that one, so I could fly to where my sister is.'

"'All right, Doña Doloritas. You can go see her right now, today. Let's go back to the house so you can pack your suitcase.'

"And your mother went.

"'Goodbye, Don Pedro.'

"'Goodbye, Doloritas.'

"She left the Media Luna for good. A few months afterwards I asked Pedro Páramo about her.

"'She likes her sister better than me. She's probably happy now. Anyway, I was getting tired of her. I'm not going to inquire about her, if that's what you're thinking.'

"'But what will they live on?'

"'Let God help them out.'"

"... *But make him pay you for having abandoned us* ..."

"And until now when she told me you were coming to see me, we didn't hear another thing about her."

"We went to live with my Aunt Gertrudis in Colima," I told her. "She kept saying what a burden we were. 'Why don't you go back to your husband?' she'd ask my mother.

"'Has he sent for me? No. I won't go back if he doesn't send for me. I came here because I wanted to see you. Because you're my sister, that's why.'

"'I understand. But it's time you went back ...'"

I thought that woman was listening to me, but she had her head cocked as if she heard some faraway murmur. Then she said:

"When are you going to get some rest?"

The day you went away, I knew I would never see you again. Your face was dark in the blood-red light of the setting sun. You were smiling. You left the village behind you, and how often you had told me: "I like it because of you, but I hate it for everything else. Even for having been born in it." I thought: "She is not coming back." And I told myself many times: "Susana is not coming back. Susana is never coming back."

"What are you doing here? Aren't you working?"

"No, Grandmother. Rogelio wants me to watch the baby, and I'm taking him for a walk. It's a hard job to watch both the telegraph and the baby, with Rogelio just drinking beer in the billiard parlor. Besides, he doesn't pay me anything."

"You aren't there to get paid, you're there to learn. When you know a little something, then you can start asking for pay. Right now you're just an apprentice. Maybe tomorrow or the day after you'll be the boss. But you've got to have patience, and learn how to take orders. If he tells you to take the baby for a walk, then do it, for the love of God. You've got to resign yourself."

"That's all right for other people, Grandmother. Not for me."

"You and your ideas! I'm afraid you're going to turn out bad, Pedro Páramo."

"What is it, Doña Eduviges?"

She shook her head, as if she were waking up from a dream. "It's Miguel Páramo's horse. On the road from the Media Luna."

"Then somebody does live in the Media Luna?"

"No, nobody lives there."

"Well, then?"

"It's just that horse of his, coming and going the way it does. They were inseparable. It runs everywhere looking for him, and it always comes back at this hour. Perhaps the poor thing can't stand its grief. Why is it that even animals know when they've committed a crime?"

"I don't understand. I didn't hear any horse."

"No? Then it must have been my sixth sense. That's a gift God gave me . . . or a punishment, perhaps. You couldn't know how much I've suffered from it."

I didn't say anything, and after a moment she added: "It all began with my godchild Miguel Páramo. I'm the only one who knew what happened the night he died. I was already in bed when I heard his horse coming back from the Media Luna. I was surprised because he never came back at that hour, always at daybreak. He'd go to talk with his girlfriend in a village called Contla, but this time he didn't come back. . . . Now do you hear it? Listen."

"I can't hear anything."

"Then it's just me again. Well, as I was saying, he didn't come back this time is what they think, but he came back. His horse hadn't gone all the way past when I heard a tapping at the window. You'll see if it was just my imagination. The truth is that something made me go to the window to see who it was. And it was Miguel Páramo. I wasn't surprised to see him, because there was a time when he'd spend the night here, sleeping with me, until he met that girl that drove him crazy.

" 'What happened?' I asked him. 'Did she throw you over?'

" 'No, she still loves me. The trouble is I couldn't find her. I couldn't even find the village. There was a lot of smoke or fog or something, but it wasn't that. Contla doesn't exist any more. I looked everywhere for it, and I didn't find anything. I came to tell you about it because you understand me. If I told anybody else in Comala, they'd just say I'm crazy, the way they do anyway.'

" 'No. You're not crazy, Miguel. You're dead. Remember they told you that horse would kill you some day, Miguel Páramo. You used to do some crazy things, but this is something else.'

" 'All I did was jump that stone wall my father had them build a while back. I made El Colorado jump it so I wouldn't have to go all the way around before getting onto the road. We jumped it and kept on going, but there wasn't anything except smoke and smoke and smoke.'

" 'Your father is going to suffer tomorrow, when he knows. I'm sorry for him. Now go rest in peace, Miguel. I'm glad you came by and woke me up.'

"And I closed the window. One of the hands from the Media Luna came to the house before dawn and said, 'Don Pedro is asking for you. Miguel is dead. He wants you to keep him company.'

" 'I know about it,' I said. 'Did they ask you to mourn?'

" 'Yes, Don Fulgor told me there ought to be mourning.'

" 'That's right. Tell Don Pedro I'll come. How long ago did they bring in the body?'

" 'Only about half an hour ago. If they'd found him sooner they might have saved him . . . though the doctor says he's been dead for a long time. We knew something happened because El Colorado came back alone and made so much noise that nobody could sleep. You know how Miguel and that horse loved each other. I almost think the horse feels worse than Don Pedro. It won't eat or sleep and just keeps wandering around, as if it knew. As if it felt broken up inside.'

" 'Don't forget to close the door when you go,' I said, and the hand from the Media Luna went away.

"Have you ever heard the groan of a dead man?" she asked me.

"No, Doña Eduviges."

"You're better off."

The drops fell from the trough, one by one. You could hear the clear water fall from the stone brim into the water jar. You could hear murmurs, and feet that scraped the ground, that walked, that came and went. The drops kept falling and falling. The water jar overflowed, and the water ran onto the wet earth.

"Wake up!"

The voice sounded familiar. He tried to guess who it was, but his body slackened and dozed off again, crushed by the weight of sleep. Hands reached out to grasp the covers, and his body hid under their warmth, seeking peace.

"Wake up!"

The voice shook him by the shoulders, and his body straightened out. He half-opened his eyes. The drops of water fell from the trough into the water jar. You could hear dragging steps . . . and the weeping. He heard the weeping. That woke him up, that soft, thin sound of weeping, perhaps because it was so thin it could slip through the mazes of sleep to the place where the fears dwell.

He got up slowly, and saw the face of a woman who leaned

against the frame of the door, still shadowy in the darkness, sobbing. As he put his feet on the floor, he recognized her.

"Why are you crying, Mamá?"

"Your father is dead."

And then, as if the coiled springs of her grief had broken loose, she said the same thing over again, over and over again, until hands grasped her shoulders and stopped her trembling.

Daylight showed through the door. There were no stars, only a leaden sky, not cleared yet by the shining of the sun; only a dark light, as if the day were not going to come, as if the night were falling.

Outside in the patio there was the sound of steps back and forth, back and forth, and hushed noises. And here, that woman standing in the shadow, holding back the day with her body, letting scraps of the sky peer in past her arms, and trickles of light at her feet, as if the ground under her were sprinkled with tears. And then the sobbing. And the weeping again, soft but sharp, and the grief that twisted her body.

"They've killed your father."

"And who killed you, Mother?"

"There is air and sunlight. There are white clouds. There is a blue sky, and perhaps there are songs beyond it, and sweeter voices. . . . There is hope, in a word. There is hope for us in our suffering.

"But not for you, Miguel Páramo. You have died in sin and you can never receive God's grace."

Father Rentería turned from the corpse and said the service for the dead. He hurried the end of it, so as to leave without giving the benediction to the people filling the church.

"Father, we would like you to bless him."

"No!" He shook his head. "I won't do it. He was an evil man. He can't enter the Kingdom of Heaven, and God would be angry with me if I interceded for him."

While he said that, he was clasping his hands together so that their trembling would not be seen.

But it was.

The corpse weighed heavily on the souls of everybody there. It was set up on a platform in the middle of the church, surrounded with flowers and new candles. Near it, all alone, his father waited for the service to end.

Father Rentería passed close to Pedro Páramo, trying not to brush against his shoulders. He raised the holy water and sprinkled it up and down with smooth gestures, while a murmur that could have been prayers issued from his mouth. Afterwards he knelt, and everybody knelt with him.

"Lord, have mercy on your servant."

"May he rest in peace, amen," the voices answered.

When he began to feel his anger rising again, he saw everybody leaving the church with the body of Miguel Páramo.

Pedro Páramo came over to him, kneeling at his side. "I know you hated him, Father. And I don't blame you. They say it was my son who killed your brother. You think he also violated your niece Ana. And sometimes he was disrespectful to you, or even offensive. Anybody would have to admit those are good reasons. But forget them now, Father. Forgive him, as perhaps God has forgiven him already."

He placed a fistful of gold coins on the bench and stood up. "Take this as a gift for the church."

The church was empty. Two men waited at the door for

Pedro Páramo. He joined them and together they followed after the coffin, which rested on the shoulders of four men from the Media Luna.

Father Rentería picked up the coins one by one, and approached the altar.

"They are Yours," he said. "He can buy salvation, and You know if this is the price of it. As for me, Lord, I'm here at Your feet to ask You for justice, or for injustice, since everything is given us to ask . . .

"For my part, send him to Hell, Lord."

He walked into the sacristy and sat down in a corner, weeping for shame and sorrow, until he exhausted all his tears.

"It is well, Lord. . . . You win," he said.

At supper he drank his usual cup of chocolate. He felt calm now.

"Listen, Ana. Do you know who was buried today?"

"No, Uncle."

"Do you remember Miguel Páramo?"

"Yes, Uncle."

"Well, Miguel."

Ana lowered her head.

"Are you sure he was the one, Ana?"

"I'm not sure, Uncle . . . I didn't see his face. He came at night."

"Then how did you know it was Miguel Páramo?"

"Because he said, 'I'm Miguel Páramo, Ana. Don't be afraid.'

That's just what he said."

"But you knew he killed your father, didn't you?"

"Yes, Uncle."

"Then what did you do to get away from him?"

"I didn't do anything."

They were silent for a moment, hearing the warm wind rustling the myrtle leaves.

"He told me the reason he came was to ask me to forgive him. 'The window is open,' I told him without getting out of bed. And he came in.

"Then he started to hug me, as if that was how I'd forgive him for what he'd done. I smiled, because I remembered what you taught me, that we shouldn't hate anybody. I smiled at him so he'd know, but then I remembered he couldn't see me in the darkness, any more than I could see him. I could only feel him on top of me, and then he began to do bad things with me.

"I thought he was going to kill me. That's just what I thought, Uncle. I tried to die before he could kill me, but I couldn't, and I guess he didn't dare to. I knew it when I opened my eyes and saw the sun coming in the open window. Before that, I thought I was dead."

"But you've got to be sure. His voice . . . didn't you know him by his voice?"

"I didn't know him by anything. I just knew he killed my father. I hadn't ever seen him before, Uncle, and I never saw him afterwards."

"But you knew who it was."

"Yes. If he was the one, he's in the deepest pit in Hell, because that's what I begged the saints with all my heart."

"You mustn't be too sure of that, child. You don't know how

many people are praying for him, and you're just one . . . one prayer against a thousand. And some of them a lot stronger than yours, like his father's."

He was going to tell her, "Besides, I've already forgiven him." But he only thought it. He didn't want to hurt her half-broken soul any further. Instead, he took her arm and said, "Let's thank Our Lord that He took him off this earth where he did so much harm. It doesn't matter if He has him up there in Heaven."

A horse galloped past the crossroad where the main street meets the road to Contla. Nobody saw it. Nevertheless, a woman who was waiting on the outskirts of town reported that she saw the horse running with its legs bent as if it were going to fall face downwards. She recognized it as Miguel Páramo's roan, and thought: "That animal is going to bash its head in." Then she saw it straighten up and run with its head turned back over its shoulder, as if it were running away from something that frightened it back there along the road.

Her story reached the Media Luna on the night of the burial, while the men were resting up from the long journey out to the graveyard. They were talking, the way people talk anywhere, before going to sleep.

"This death really hurt me," Terencio Lubianes said. "My shoulders are still sore."

"Mine too," his brother Ubillado said. "And my bunions are twice as big as they were before. But the Boss made us all put shoes on . . . and it wasn't even a holiday, either. Isn't that right, Toribio?"

"I don't care what anybody says, I think he died right on time."

A little later, more news arrived from Contla, with the last wagon.

"They say his spirit is walking there. They've seen it knocking at what's-her-name's window. It looks exactly like him, with chaps and everything."

"Do you think Don Pedro would let his son keep chasing the whores? Not with that temper of his. I can just hear what he'd say if he knew about it: 'Look,' he'd say, 'you're dead now. So stay in your grave where you belong, and leave this business to the rest of us.' And if he saw him walking around alive, I bet he'd send him out to the graveyard again."

"You're right, Isaías. The old man doesn't put up with any nonsense."

There were falling stars. They fell as if the sky were raining fire.

"Look," Terencio said, "what a show up there."

"That's because they're celebrating for Miguel," Jesús said.

"It isn't a bad sign."

"Why?"

"Maybe your sister wants him to come back."

"Who are you talking to?"

"You."

"Let's go. We've worked hard, and it's almost morning."

And they dissolved like shadows.

But still somebody shouted, "Tell your sister not to cry, there's always me."

"Give my regards to yours, too."

There were falling stars. The lights of Comala went out one by one, and the sky took possession of the night.

Father Rentería turned in his bed, unable to sleep. Everything that happened is my fault, he told himself. Afraid to offend the people who have money. Because they give me my living. I never get anything from the poor. And prayers don't fill your stomach. That's how it's been up till now. And these are the consequences. My fault. I've betrayed everybody who loves me, and they still trust in me and ask me to intercede for them with God. But what have they got for their trust? The key to Heaven? The cleansing of their souls? And why should they cleanse their souls if at the last moment. . . . I can still see María Dyada when she came to ask me if I'd save her sister Eduviges:

"She was always serving her fellow human beings. She gave them everything she had. She even gave them sons, all of them. She'd show them her children so they'd admit they were theirs, but they wouldn't admit it. She told her children, 'In that case I'm your father too, even though I'm your mother.' Everybody took advantage of her, just because she was so good she didn't want to offend them or quarrel with them.

"But she committed suicide. That's against the will of God.

"There was nothing else she could do . . . and she did that, too, because she was so good.

"'You failed at the last moment,' I told her. 'At the very last moment. You had all those good deeds saved up for your salvation . . . and then to throw them all away!'

"But she didn't throw them away. She died full of grief. And grief . . . you've told us something about grief, Father, but I can't remember. That's how she died, with the blood choking her. I can still see her expressions. They were the most pitiful expressions a human being ever made.

"Perhaps by praying a lot. . . . Let's pray a lot, Father. I say 'perhaps.' Perhaps with Gregorian Masses we could. . . . But we'll need help for those, we'll have to send for priests. And that costs money."

There before my eyes was María Dyada, a poor woman with many children.

"I don't have any money. You know that, Father."

"Let's leave things as they are. Let's trust in God."

"Yes, Father."

What would it have cost him to grant forgiveness, when it was so easy to mumble a word or two, or even a hundred if they were necessary to save a soul? What did he know about Heaven and Hell? Nevertheless, he knew who had deserved to go to Heaven. He was lost in a nameless village, but he knew. He had a list. He began to go over the saints of the Catholic pantheon, beginning with the saints of that day: "Santa Nunilona, virgin and martyr; Santas Salomé, widow, Alodia or Elodia and Nulina, virgins; Córdula and Donato." And he kept on. He was beginning to feel drowsy as he sat on the edge of the bed: "I'm counting saints as if I were counting sheep."

He went outside and looked at the sky. It was raining stars. He regretted that, because he wanted to see a tranquil sky. He heard the crowing of the cocks, and felt the shroud of night covering the earth . . .

The earth, "this vale of tears."

"You're better off, my son," Eduviges Dyada told me. "You're better off."

It was late at night by now. The lamp in the corner began to dim, then it flickered and went out.

I heard her get up, and I thought she was going for another light. I heard her footsteps moving away. I waited for her.

She didn't come back, and after a while I got up too. I walked with short steps, feeling my way along in the darkness, till I came to my room. I sat down on the floor to wait till I felt sleepy.

I slept, but only off and on.

It was during a waking spell that I heard the shout. It was the kind of shout a drunkard would give: "The hell with life anyway!"

I sat bolt upright because it was so loud it seemed right at my ear. It could have been out in the street, but I was sure it was inside, next to the walls of my room. But then there was nothing, just the flutter of a moth and the murmurs of the silence.

It was impossible to calculate the depth of the silence that shout created. As if the earth had been emptied of air. No sound, not even the sound of my breathing, or my heart beating. And when the moment had passed, and I was beginning to calm down, the shout came back and remained for a long time: "Let me kick! You can hang me, but let me kick!"

Suddenly the door opened.

"Is that you, Doña Eduviges?" I asked. "What's happening? Are you frightened?"

"My name isn't Eduviges. I'm Damiana. I knew you were here and I've come to see you. I want to invite you to sleep at my house. You can sleep better there."

"Damiana Cisneros? Didn't you live in the Media Luna?"

"That's where I live. That's why it took me so long to get here."

"My mother told me about a Damiana that used to take care of me when I was a baby. Are you . . ."

"Yes, I am. I've known you ever since you first opened your eyes."

"I'll go with you. I can't get to sleep here with all the shouting. Didn't you hear what was going on? As if they were murdering somebody?"

"Perhaps it was an echo that got locked in here. They hanged Toribio Aldrete in this room, a long time ago. Then they locked the door and let his body dry up, so he'd never find rest. I don't know how you got in, when there isn't any key to the door."

"Doña Eduviges opened it. She told me it was the only room she could give me."

"Eduviges Dyada?"

"Yes."

"Poor Eduviges. Then she must still be suffering."

"I, Fulgor Sedano, age 54, single, profession manager, empowered to initiate and settle lawsuits, charge and assert the following . . ."

This is what he said when he presented the claim against Toribio Aldrete. And he concluded: "The charge consists in usufrock."

"Nobody can say you're not a real man, Don Fulgor. I know you can do what you claim. Not just because you've got authority behind you. Because you're the man you are, that's why."

Don Fulgor agreed. The first thing Aldrete told him, after they started getting drunk to celebrate the settlement, was: "We're covered by this paper, Don Fulgor, because it's not going to be any good for anything else. You know that. As far as you're concerned, you've done what they sent you to do . . . and you've got me out of trouble. You had me worried at first, though. Now that I know what it's all about, I have to laugh. 'Usufrock,' it says. Your boss ought to be ashamed of himself for being so ignorant."

Don Fulgor agreed. They were in the rooming-house of Eduviges Dyada, and he asked her, "Listen, Viges, will you let me use your corner room?"

"Any one you want, Don Fulgor. You can use all of them if you want to. Are your men going to sleep here tonight?"

"No, just one. Go to bed and don't worry about us. Just leave us the key."

"So that's what I tell you, Don Fulgor," Toribio Aldrete said. "Nobody can say you aren't a real man. But I can't stand that fucking slob you've got for a boss."

Don Fulgor agreed. It was the last coherent thing he heard him say, because later he behaved like a coward, shouting and shouting. He said to him: "The authority I've got behind me, eh? Well, now!"

He knocked with his whip handle at the door of Pedro Páramo's house, and thought of the first time he had knocked there, two weeks earlier. He waited a good while, just as he had waited that first time. He also saw once again the piece of black cloth that hung over the door. But he didn't talk to himself the way he had before: "So they've put up another one. The first one's all faded, but the new one shines just like silk . . . though it's only a dyed rag."

The first time, he waited so long that he decided the house was empty. He was going to go away when the figure of Pedro Páramo appeared.

It was the second occasion he had seen him. On that first occasion Pedro was only a baby. And now this time. You could almost say this was the first occasion. The result was that he began talking with him like an equal. He followed him in with long strides, saying, "You'll see I know what's what. And you'll see why I'm here."

"Sit down, Fulgor. We can talk out here without being interrupted."

They were in the back yard. Pedro Páramo sprawled out on a box and waited. "Why don't you sit down?"

"I'd rather stand up, Pedro."

"As you like. But don't forget the 'Don.'"

Who was this boy to speak to him like that? His father, Don Lucas Páramo, had never insulted him like that, and here was this Pedro, who hardly knew anything about the Media Luna or how it was run, treating him like a farm hand.

"How are things going?"

He felt that his opportunity had arrived. "Now it's my turn," he said to himself.

"Worse and worse. There isn't anything left. We've sold the last animal."

He began to take papers out of his pocket to tell him what the debt was, and he was going to say, "We owe thus and so," when Pedro Páramo said:

"Who do we owe it to? I don't care how much, just who."

He read off a list of names. "And there isn't anything to pay them with. That's the problem."

"Why?"

"Because your family used everything up. They kept taking and taking and never gave anything back. I said to myself, 'Sooner or later they'll take everything.' Well, they did. Though there are people who would buy the land, and pay well. The debts could be paid off with the money, and there would still be something left. But not very much."

"It wouldn't be you?"

"How could it possibly be me?"

"Tomorrow we'll start to work. The Preciados first. Didn't you say we owe them the most?"

"Yes. And we've paid them the least. Your father always planned to pay them last of all. I think one of them, Matilde, went to live in the city, but I don't know if it was Guadalajara or Colima. And Lola . . . I mean Doña Dolores . . . is the owner of everything. You know, the Enmedio farm. And she's the one we have to pay."

"Tomorrow you're going to propose to Lola."

"She wouldn't even look at me. I'm too old."

"Propose for me. Tell her I'm very much in love with her. And while you're at it, tell Father Rentería to arrange for the wedding. How much money have you got?"

"None, Don Pedro."

"Promise it, then. Tell him it'll be paid. I don't think there'll be any trouble. Do that tomorrow."

"And what about Toribio Aldrete?"

"What about him? You mentioned the Preciados and the Fregosos and the Guzmanes. What's this about Aldrete?"

"It's a question of boundaries. He's putting up fences and he wants us to put up our part, to finish dividing."

"Leave that till later . . . and don't worry about boundaries. There won't be any. Remember that, Fulgor, even if you don't understand it. The land won't be divided. Now arrange that business about Lola. Don't you want to sit down?"

"Thank you, Don Pedro, I will. I certainly do like working with you."

"Tell Lola this and that and the other thing, but tell her I love her. That's important. And it's true, Sedano, I do love her. For her eyes, you know. So arrange that business tomorrow. I'll reduce some of your duties as manager. You can forget about the Media Luna."

"Where the Devil did the boy learn these tricks?" Fulgor Sedano asked himself as he walked back to the Media Luna. "I didn't expect a damned thing from him. 'He's a good-for-nothing,' his father Don Lucas said, 'just a lazy lout.' I told him he was right. 'When I'm dead, look for another job, Fulgor.' 'Yes, Don Lucas.' 'I'll tell you frankly, Fulgor, I've thought of sending him to the seminary, to see if he could at least learn enough to support his poor mother when I'm gone, but even that doesn't suit him.' 'You don't deserve all these troubles, Don Lucas.' 'Don't count on him for anything. I'm getting old and he won't even be any help to his own father. He's disappointed me, Fulgor.' 'It's a terrible thing, Don Lucas.'"

And now this. Don Pedro wasn't in love with the Media Luna before, hadn't even gone to see it, but he loved it now, all of it. All of those bare hillsides that had been farmed for so long and still yielded so much. "We're in business again," he said to himself, and he slapped his leg with the whip as he passed through the great gate of the hacienda.

It was very easy to impress Dolores. Her eyes gleamed and her excitement showed in her face.

"Excuse me for blushing, Don Fulgor. I didn't think Don Pedro ever noticed me."

"He can't sleep for thinking about you."

"But he could have his choice. There's lots of pretty girls in Comala. What will they say when they know?"

"He just thinks about you, Dolores. Not about anybody else."

"You're giving me chills and fevers, Don Fulgor. I never even imagined."

"It's just that he keeps his thoughts to himself. Don Lucas, may he rest in peace, told him you weren't suitable for him, and that's why he kept quiet, out of obedience. Now that his father has passed on, there isn't any obstacle. It was the very first decision he made on his own, although I've been a little slow about delivering the message, on account of my work. We'll set the wedding for the day after tomorrow. Is that all right?"

"Isn't it awfully soon? I don't have anything ready. I'll have to buy my trousseau, and write to my sister, and . . . no, it would be better to send a messenger. Anyhow, I won't be ready before April 8th. Today's the first. Yes, about the 8th. Ask him to give me a few more days."

"He even wanted it to be today. If you're worried about your trousseau, we'll furnish it for you. Don Pedro's dead mother hoped you'd wear her wedding gown. It's a family custom."

"But there's other things besides. Women's things, you know. But I'm ashamed to tell you, Don Fulgor. Look how I'm blushing! It's . . . it's that time of the month . . ."

"So what? Marriage isn't a question of the calendar. It's a question of love. That's more important than anything."

"You don't understand, Don Fulgor."

"I understand perfectly. The wedding will be the day after tomorrow."

And he left her with her arms stretched out, begging for one week, for just one week.

"I mustn't forget to remind Don Pedro . . . what a shrewd boy that Pedro is! . . . to tell the judge that everything is to be in his name. 'Remember to tell him tomorrow, Fulgor.'"

Dolores ran to the kitchen with a water jug to heat some water. "I'll make it go away sooner. Tonight, if I can. But it won't, it'll last three days. There's no helping it. Dear God, how happy I am! I thank You for giving me to Don Pedro!"

And she added: "Even if he gets tired of me later."

"I asked her and she's completely agreeable. The priest wants sixty pesos to forget about the marriage banns. I told him he'd be paid at the proper time. He also said he needs money to decorate the altar. I said all right. And it seems that his dining table is falling apart. I said we'd send him a new table. He said you never go to Mass. I promised that you'd go. Finally he said you haven't paid your tithes since your grandmother died. I told him not to worry. He won't be any problem."

"Did you ask Dolores for something in advance?"

"No, *patrón*. I didn't quite dare. She was so happy, I didn't want to spoil anything."

"Fulgor, you're a child."

A child? Go away! I'm 55. He's hardly begun to live, and I'm just a few steps from the grave.

"I didn't want to spoil her happiness."

"All the same, you're a child."

"All right, *patrón*."

"The next thing is Aldrete. Tell him he went beyond the boundaries. He's invaded lands that belong to the Media Luna."

"But he measured it carefully. I think he's right."

"Tell him he made a mistake, he didn't measure correctly. Knock the fences down if you have to."

"And the law?"

"What law, Fulgor? From now on we're going to make the laws ourselves. Do you have any good tough men in the Media Luna?"

"Yes. A few."

"Take them along when you go see Aldrete. Accuse him of usufrock, or anything else that occurs to you. And remind him that Lucas Páramo is dead now. He's got to make new arrangements with me."

The sky was still blue, with a few clouds. The wind was blowing up above, but down below there was nothing but heat.

He knocked again with the handle of his whip, merely to insist, now that he knew they wouldn't open the door till it suited Don Pedro's whim. He looked up over the doorway and said to himself, "That black cloth looks fine, no matter what."

At that moment the door opened, and he went in.

"Fulgor, have you arranged that business about Toribio Aldrete?"

"It's all taken care of, *patrón*."

"That leaves the question of the Fregosos. Let it wait a little. Right now I'm very busy with my honeymoon."

"The village is full of echoes. Perhaps they got trapped in the hollows of the walls, or under the stones. When you walk in the street you can hear other footsteps, and rustling noises, and laughter. Old laughter, as if it were tired of laughing by now. And voices worn out with use. You can hear all this. I think someday these sounds will die away."

That is what Damiana Cisneros was telling me as we crossed the village.

"I remember the time I could hear the sounds of a fiesta night after night. I could even hear them out in the Media Luna. I went to the plaza to see what was happening, and I saw what we're seeing right now. Nothing. Not a soul. The streets were as empty as they are right now.

"Then I stopped hearing it. Even happiness gets tired after a while. That's why I wasn't surprised when it ended.

"Yes, the village is full of echoes. They don't scare me any more. I hear the dogs howling and I let them howl, because I know there aren't any dogs here any more. And on windy days you can hear the wind shaking the leaves, but you already know there aren't any trees. There must have been trees here once, or where would the leaves have come from?

"And the worst thing of all is when you hear people talking, as if their voices came out of some crack in the street or the walls, although they're so clear you can even recognize them. Just tonight I came across a wake. I stopped to say a paternoster, and while I was saying it a woman left the others and came over to me. 'Damiana! Pray for me, Damiana!'

"She opened her rebozo and I saw she was my sister Sixtina.

" 'What are you doing here?' I asked her.

"Then she ran back to hide among the other women.

"You wouldn't know, but my sister Sixtina died when I was twelve years old. She was the oldest. There were sixteen of us in the family, so you can imagine how long she's been dead. And look at her now, still wandering the earth. So don't be frightened if you hear echoes, Juan Preciado."

"Did my mother tell you I was coming?" I asked her.

"No. What happened to your mother?"

"She died," I said.

"Oh? What from?"

"I don't know. Sorrow, perhaps. She was always sighing."

"That's bad. Every time you sigh, a little bit of your life goes out of you. Is that how she died?"

"Yes. I thought you'd know."

"How was I going to know? I haven't known anything for years now."

"Then how did you know I was here?"

She was silent.

"Are you alive, Damiana? Tell me, Damiana!"

Suddenly I found myself alone in those empty streets. The windows of the houses were open to the night, with the weeds peering out of them. The walls were peeling, showing their rotted adobes.

"Damiana! Damiana Cisneros!"

And the echoes answered me: ". . . Ana . . . neros. . . !
. . . Ana . . . neros. . . !"

I could hear the dogs barking, as if I had wakened them. I saw a man cross the street.

"You!" I called.

"You!" he called back. In my own voice.

And I could hear women gossiping, as if they were just around the corner.

"Look who's coming. Isn't that Filoteo Aréchiga?"

"Yes. Don't let him see what you're thinking."

"Let's go home. If he's following us, it means he wants one of us. Who do you think he wants?"

"You."

"I think he wants you."

"Look, he's stopped. He's just standing there at the corner."

"Then he wasn't following either one of us."

"What would have happened if he was?"

"Don't start imagining."

"They say he's the one who brings girls for Don Pedro."

"I don't want to have anything to do with him."

"Let's go."

"Good, let's go."

The night. Long after midnight. And the voices.

". . . I tell you I'll pay you if the corn crop is good this year. If it isn't, you'll just have to wait."

"I'm not pressing you. You know how patient I've been. But the land isn't yours. You've farmed somebody else's land. So how are you going to pay me?"

"Who says it isn't my land?"

"They say you sold it to Pedro Páramo."

"I've never even been near him. The land is mine."

"You can say so, but I'm told it's all his now."

"Just let them say that to me!"

"Look, Galileo, I'll tell you frankly, I like you. For one thing, you're my sister's husband, and I know you take good care of her. But please don't try to deny that you sold the land."

"I tell you I haven't sold it to anybody."

"But it belongs to Pedro Páramo. He must have wanted it. Hasn't Fulgor Sedano been to see you?"

"No."

"Well, he'll show up tomorrow. Or the day after tomorrow. He'll show up."

"Let him. Let him kill me if he can. But I'll kill him too."

"Requiescat and pace. Amen."

"You'll see, you'll see! Don't worry about me. My mother didn't tan my hide to make a coward out of me."

"All right, then. Tell Felícitas I won't come by for supper tonight. I wouldn't want to say later, 'I was with him that evening.' "

"All right. But we'll save something for you, in case you change your mind."

Footsteps. The jingle of spurs. Vanishing away.

". . . We'll leave at dawn tomorrow, Chona. I've got the mules all harnessed."

"And if my father dies of anger? He's so old. . . . I'd never forgive myself if anything happened to him on my account. I'm the only person he's got to take care of him. There isn't anybody else. Why are you in such a hurry to take me away? Wait a little bit. He won't live very long."

"That's what you told me a year ago. You even told me I was afraid of the risk, as if you were ready for anything. I've paid for the mules in advance, everything's ready. Will you go with me?"

"Let me think about it."

"Chona, don't you know how much I love you? I can't wait any longer, Chona. You'll have to go with me."

"Give me time to think. We have to wait till he dies. It won't be very long. Then I'll go with you and you won't have to steal me."

"You told me that a year ago, too."

"And?"

"But I had to hire the mules. I've got them now. They're waiting. Let him get along by himself! You're young and beautiful. He'll find some old woman to take care of him. There's lots of kind souls here in the village."

"I can't."

"Yes, you can."

"I can't. I can't, don't you understand? He's still my father."

"Then there's nothing left to say. I'll go see Juliana. She's dying for me."

"All right. I can't say anything more."

"You don't want to see me tomorrow?"

"No. I don't ever want to see you again."

Noises. Voices. Murmurs. Faraway songs.

> *My love gave me a handkerchief*
> *With a border of tears . . .*

In falsetto, as if those who sang them were women.

I saw the wagons passing. The oxen slowly passing. The sound of the wheels on the stones. The men as if they were asleep.

"*. . . Every morning at dawn the village trembles with the rumbling of the wagons. They come in from everywhere, loaded with saltpeter, with corn, with hay. The wheels creak and creak, rattling the windows and waking up the village. That's the hour when the ovens are opened and the air smells of new-baked bread. Suddenly it thunders, perhaps, and the rain falls. Perhaps spring is coming. You'll learn there what 'perhaps' means, my son . . .*"

Empty wagons, shattering the silence of the streets. Vanishing down the dark roads of the night. And the shadows. And the echo of the shadows.

I thought of going back. I knew that up there was the gap I had come through, like an open wound in the blackness of the mountains.

Then somebody touched me on the shoulder.

"What are you doing here?"

"I came here to look for . . ." I was about to tell him, but I caught myself. "To look for my father."

"Why don't you come in?"

I went in. It was a house with half of the roof fallen in, roof-tiles scattered over the floor, the roof on the floor. And in the other half a man and a woman.

"Are you dead?" I asked them.

The woman laughed. The man looked at me solemnly.

"He's drunk," he said.

"No, he's just frightened," the woman said.

There was an oil lamp, a crude bed, and a chair with the woman's clothes on it. Because she was as naked as when God sent her into the world. So was he.

"We heard somebody moaning and beating his head against the door. And there you were. What happened?"

"I can't tell you now. I want to sleep."

"We were already asleep."

"Let's go to sleep, then."

The dawn dimmed my memories.

From time to time I heard the sound of words, and noticed the difference. The words I had heard up till then didn't have any sound, they were silent words you could sense but not hear, like those in a dream.

"Who is he?" the woman asked.

"Who knows?"

"Why did he come here?"

"Who knows?"

"I heard him say something about his father."

"So did I."

"Do you think he's lost? Remember those others that came here when they got lost? They told you they were looking for a place called Los Confines. You said you didn't know where it was."

"Yes, I remember. But let me sleep, it still isn't daylight."

"It will be pretty soon. That's why I'm talking to you, so you'll stay awake. You told me last night to wake you up before dawn. That's why. Get up."

"Why do you want me to get up?"

"I don't know. You just told me to wake you up. You didn't say why."

"In that case, let me sleep. Didn't you hear what he said when he came in, to let him sleep? That was the only thing he said."

As if the voices were vanishing. As if they were losing their sound. As if they were choked off. Nobody said a word. It was a dream.

And then, a little later: "He moved. I think he's going to wake up. If he sees us here he'll ask us things."

"What can he ask us?"

"You know. And he'll be sure to say something, won't he?"

"Let him. He must be awfully tired."

"Do you think so?"

"Be quiet, woman."

"Look, he just moved again. Did you see how he turned over? As if his conscience is hurting him. I know, because the same thing has happened to me."

"What's happened to you?"

"The same thing."

"I don't know what you're talking about."

"I wouldn't be talking if he didn't make me remember what happened to me the first time you did it. And how it hurt me and how I repented it."

"What?"

"The way I felt as soon as you did it. You want me to forget about it, but I can't."

"Are you still thinking about that? Why don't you let me sleep?"

"You told me to wake you up. That's what I'm doing. God knows I'm only doing what you told me. Come on, get up. It's past time."

"Let me alone, woman."

The man seemed to be asleep. The woman kept on mumbling, but in a very low voice.

"It must be dawn already, because there's light. I can see that man from here, and I couldn't see him if there weren't any light. The sun will come up any minute now. If you ask me, he's probably committed some crime . . . and we let him hide out here. It doesn't make any difference that it was just for one night: we hid him. This will probably get us in trouble. Look at the way he moves, as if he couldn't get comfortable. He must have something bad on his conscience."

The day dawned, scattering the shadows. The room felt warm from the heat of the sleeping bodies. The first light touched my eyelids. I felt the light. I heard:

"He's twisting around like a soul in torment. He has all the signs of a bad man. Get up, Donis! Look at him! He's twisting around and scratching at the floor. Look, he's drooling now! He must have killed a lot of people. And you invited him in."

"He's probably just poor. Go to sleep."

"Why should I go to sleep? I'm not sleepy."

"Then get up and go somewhere where you won't be such a nuisance!"

"All right. I'll light the fire. And I'll tell what's-his-name to come lie down with you in my place."

"Tell him, then."

"I can't. I'm afraid of him."

"Then go do your work and let us alone."

"All right."

"What are you waiting for?"

"Nothing."

I could tell that the woman was getting out of bed. Her bare feet moved across the dirt floor and passed over my head. I opened and closed my eyes.

When I woke up it was noon. There was a mug of coffee beside me. I drank a few swallows of it.

"We don't have anything else. We're short of everything . . ."

It was the voice of the woman.

"Don't worry about me," I said. "I'm used to being hungry. How do you leave here?"

"To go where?"

"Anywhere."

"There's lots of roads. One of them goes to Contla, and another one comes in from there. Then there's another one that goes straight over the sierra. The one you can see from here . . ." —and she pointed out of the gap in the tiles where the roof was broken—"I don't know where it goes. That one over there goes to the Media Luna. And there's still another, that goes farther than any of them."

"Perhaps that's the one I came in on."

"Where does it go?"

"To Sayula."

"Imagine that! I thought Sayula was nearer here. I've always wanted to go there. They say there's lots of people there."

"The same as anywhere."

"Think of that! And we're so all alone here. Wanting to know a little something of life."

"Where did your husband go?"

"He isn't my husband, he's my brother . . . although he doesn't want anybody to know it. Where did he go? To look for a calf that strayed away. At least that's what he told me."

"How long have you lived here?"

"Always. We were born here."

"You must have known Dolores Preciado."

"Maybe Donis did. I hardly know anybody. I never go out. I've been here forever, right here where you see me. . . . No, that's not true. Just since he made me his woman. Since then I've stayed inside, so they won't see me. He won't believe it, but isn't it true I'm ugly?" She came over into the sunlight. "Look at my face!"

It was a common, ordinary face.

"What is it you want me to see?"

"Can't you see my sins? Can't you see those purple stains, like impetigo? And that's only on the outside. Inside I'm a sea of mud."

"But who's going to notice anything if there isn't anybody here? I've been through the whole village and I haven't seen anybody at all."

"That's the way it looks, but there's still a few. Filomeno is still alive, isn't he? And Dorotea, and Melquiades, and old Prudencio, and Sóstenes, aren't they all alive? But they stay inside. I don't know what they do in the daytime, but at night they stay inside. The nights are sheer terror. If you could just see all the souls that walk loose in the streets. . . . As soon as it gets dark they start coming out, and we're all afraid of seeing them. There's so many of them, and so few of us, we don't even try to pray for them so their souls can rest. Our prayers aren't enough for all of them. Perhaps a bit of the paternoster might reach them, but it wouldn't do them any good. We're too full of sin. There isn't one of us living here who's in the grace of God. We can't even raise our eyes without feeling them burn with shame. And shame doesn't cure anything. At least that's what the bishop said when he came by here a while back for the confirmations. I went up to him and confessed everything.

" 'That can't be pardoned,' he said.

" 'I'm filled with shame.'

" 'That isn't the remedy.'

" 'Marry us!'

" 'Leave him!'

"I wanted to tell him that life had brought us together, had captured us and tied us to each other. We were so alone here that we were the only ones. And the village had to be populated somehow. Perhaps when he came back we'd have someone for him to confirm.

"'Leave him. That's the only thing you can do.'"

"'But how will we live?'"

"'Like human beings.'"

"And he rode away with a grim face, without looking back, as if he were leaving Hell itself behind him. He's never returned. So that's why the village is full of spirits, a whole throng of wandering souls that died in sin and can't find any way of getting pardon, least of all with our help. . . . Here he is. Can you hear him?"

"Yes."

"It's Donis."

The door opened.

"What happened to the calf?" she asked.

"It didn't come back, but I followed its tracks. I think I know where it is. I'll catch it tonight."

"Are you going to leave me alone in the night?"

"Why not?"

"I couldn't stand it. I have to have you here. It's the only time I feel calm. At night."

"But I'm going after the calf tonight."

"I just found out," I said, "that you're her brother."

"I told him so he'd understand. That's the only reason."

"What do you understand, then?"

She went over to him, leaned on his shoulders, and said, "Yes, what is it you understand?"

"Nothing," I said. "I keep understanding less and less." And I added, "I want to go back where I came from. There's still a little light."

"No, you'd better wait," the man said. "You can go tomorrow.

It's almost nightfall and the roads are full of brambles. You could get lost. I'll show you the way tomorrow."

"All right," I said.

I could see flocks of blackbirds through the break in the roof. They always fly home at dusk, before the darkness closes down. And a few clouds, broken up by the wind that comes to take away the day. Later the evening star came out, and then the moon.

The man and the woman were away. They went out the door to the patio and didn't come back till it was already night. So they didn't know what happened while they were outside.

A woman came into the room from the street. She was old and terribly thin. She came in and looked all around the room. Perhaps she saw me. Perhaps she thought I was asleep. She went straight to the bed and took a box out from under it, and searched through it. She put some sheets under her arm and went out on tiptoe as if she were afraid of waking me up.

I kept very still, holding my breath, trying not to watch. Finally I turned my head and looked over there where the evening star was shining next to the moon.

"Drink this!"

I didn't dare turn my head.

"Drink it, it's good for you. It's orange-blossom tea. I know you're frightened, because you're trembling. This will help you feel better."

I recognized her hands, and when I raised my eyes I recognized her face. The man was standing behind her, and he asked me, "Do you feel sick?"

"I don't know. I see people that you don't. A woman was just in here. You must have seen her go out."

"Leave him alone," he said to the woman. "He's a mystic."

"We should put him in the bed. Look how he's shaking. He must have a fever."

"Don't worry about him. These types just do that to get attention. I knew one of them in the Media Luna. They said he could divine the future. What he never divined was that he was going to die when the *patrón* divined his mistakes. This one must be one of those mystics. They go from village to village 'to see what Providence brings them,' but he won't even find anybody here who'll give him something to eat. Look, he's stopped trembling. That's because he's listening."

As if time had turned backward. I saw the star next to the moon again. The clouds breaking up. The flocks of blackbirds. Then the afternoon, still full of light.

The walls reflecting the afternoon sun. My footsteps on the stones. The man with the burros who told me, "Look for Doña Eduviges, if she's still alive."

Then a dark room, and a woman snoring beside me. I noticed that her breathing was uneven, as if she were dreaming, or as if she weren't really asleep, just imitating the sounds of a dream. It was a slat bed, covered with sacks that smelled of urine, as if they'd never been aired in the sun, and the pillow was made of coarse cloth stuffed with silk-cotton, or with wool so hard or sweat-soaked it was almost like wood.

I could feel the woman's naked legs next to mine, and her breath next to my face. I sat up in bed and leaned back on that adobe pillow.

"Aren't you asleep?" she asked.

"I'm not sleepy. I slept all day. Where is your brother?"

"He went out. You heard him say he was going to. He probably won't come back tonight."

"You mean he still left after what you told him?"

"Yes. I don't think he'll come back. That's the way they all start out. I've got to go here, or I've got to go over there. Till finally they go so far away it's easier just to stay there. He's always wanted to leave, and I think that's what's happened. He didn't say anything to me, but I think he left me with you, so you could take care of me. He saw his chance. All that about the stray calf was only a story. You'll see, he isn't going to come back."

I wanted to tell her, "I'm going outside to get some air, I feel sick to my stomach," but I just said, "Don't worry, he'll come back."

When I got up, she said, "I left you something on the brazier in the kitchen. It isn't very much, but it'll kill your hunger."

I found a piece of jerked beef, and some tortillas on the brazier.

"It's all I could get," I heard her saying from the other room, "I got them from my sister, for two clean sheets that I've kept since my mother died. She must have come to get them. I didn't want to say so in front of Donis, but she was the woman that frightened you."

A black sky, full of stars. And next to the moon the biggest star of all.

"Can't you hear me?" I asked in a low voice.

And her voice answered me: "Where are you?"

"Here. In your village. Among your own people. Can't you see me?"

"No, my son. I can't see you."

Her voice seemed to embrace everything. And then it was lost beyond the earth.

"No, I can't see you."

I went back to the room where that woman was sleeping.

"I'm going to stay here, in my own corner. The bed is as hard as the floor. If anything happens, tell me."

"Donis won't come back," she said. "I could tell from his eyes. He was just waiting for somebody to come here so he could go away. So now you have to take care of me . . . or don't you want to? Come here and sleep with me."

"I'm all right where I am."

"But you'll be better off in the bed. The ticks will eat you up down there."

I got up and got into bed with her.

The heat made me wake up. It was midnight. The heat and the sweat. Her body was made of earth, was covered with crusts of earth, and now it was melting into a pool of mud. I felt as if I were drowning in the sweat that streamed from her. I couldn't breathe. I got up, but the woman went on sleeping. Her mouth was open and a bubbling sound came out of it, like the death-rattle.

I went out into the street for a little air, but the heat followed me out and wouldn't go away. There wasn't any air. Only the silent, stupified night, scorched by the August dog days.

There wasn't any air. I had to swallow the same air I breathed out, holding it back with my hands so it wouldn't escape. I could feel it coming and going, and each time it was less and less, until it got so thin it slipped through my fingers forever.

Forever.

I remember seeing something like a cloud of foam, and washing myself in the foam, and losing myself in the cloud. That was the last thing I saw.

"Are you asking me to believe you died of suffocation, Juan Preciado? I found you in the plaza, a long way from Donis's house, and he was right there with me, telling me you were dying. We dragged you into the shadow of the arcade, and you were having convulsions, the way people die of fright. If there wasn't any air on the night you talk about, how did we have the strength to bring you out here and bury you? And you can see that we buried you."

"You're right, Doroteo. Didn't you tell me your name was Doroteo?"

"It's all the same. My name is really Dorotea. But it's all the same."

"You're right, Dorotea. It was the voices that killed me."

". . . *You'll see why I loved it there, my son. The village I loved. Where the dreams made me thin. My village, raised up over the fields. Full of trees and green leaves, like a money-box where we kept our memories. You'll feel that you'd like to live there forever. Daybreak, morning, afternoon, evening, always the same except for the difference in the air. The air changes the colors of everything . . .*"

"Yes, Dorotea, the voices killed me. It was because I was so frightened. I couldn't bear it any longer. I wasn't in my right mind. I remember that I went to the plaza leaning against the wall, as if I were walking with my hands. And those murmurs seemed to come from the walls, to seep out of the cracks and broken spots. They were people's voices but they weren't clear, they were almost secret, as if they were whispering something to me as I passed, or were only a buzzing in my ears. I pushed myself away from the wall and walked in the middle of the street, but I heard them just the same, as if they were going with me, in front of me or behind. And I didn't feel hot the way I told you before. I felt cold. From the time I left the house of that woman that loaned me the bed I felt cold. And I kept feeling colder and colder, till I had goose-pimples. I wanted to go back, because I thought I might find the heat I'd just left, but I could tell the cold was coming from inside me, from my own blood. Then I knew how frightened I was. I heard a louder noise from the plaza, and I thought I could calm down a little if I went there among all the people. That's why you found me in the plaza. So Donis came back after all? The woman was sure she'd never see him again."

"It was already daylight when we found you. I don't know where Donis came from. I didn't ask him."

"Well, I went to the plaza and leaned against one of the pillars in the arcade. I could see there wasn't anybody there, but I still heard the murmur of voices, as if it were market day. It was just a meaningless hum, like the sound the wind makes in the branches of a tree at night, when you can't see the tree or the branches but you can hear the rustle. Like that. I didn't go any farther. I began to sense that muttering coming nearer and

circling round me like a swarm of bees, till finally I could make
out a few words: 'Pray to God for us.' That's what they were
saying to me. Then my soul froze. That's why you found me
dead."

"You should have stayed home. Why did you want to come
here?"

"I told you at the beginning. They said that Pedro Páramo
was my father, and I came to look for him. That was the illusion
that brought me here."

"Illusions are bad. It was an illusion that made me live longer
than I should have. That's how I paid for trying to find my
son, who was only another illusion. I never had a son. Now that
I'm dead I've had time to think everything over, and I understand. God didn't even give me any home to keep him in. Just
a long, weary life, always searching wherever I went, looking
sideways, looking behind people, always suspecting they'd hidden
my child. And it was all the fault of my bad dream. I've had
two. I call one of them my bad dream and the other one my
good one. The first was the one that made me dream I'd had
a son. As long as I lived I never stopped believing it was true,
because I could feel him in my arms, I could feel his mouth and
his little hands. For a long time my fingers still had the feel of
his closed eyelids and the beating of his heart. So how could
I help but believe it? I carried him with me everywhere I went,
wrapped up in my rebozo, and suddenly I lost him. They told
me in Heaven that they'd made a mistake. They said they'd
given me the heart of a mother, but not a mother's womb.
That was the other dream I had. I arrived in Heaven and
looked all over to see if I could recognize my son's face among

the angels. It wasn't any use. Their faces were all the same, every one of them. So I asked about him. One of those saints came up to me without saying a word and buried his hand in my stomach as if he'd put it into a ball of soft wax. When he took it out again he showed me something that looked like a nutshell: 'And what I show you is the proof.'

"You know the funny way they talk up there. But you can understand them. I wanted to tell him it was only my stomach, all shriveled up from never having enough to eat, but one of the other saints put his hand on my shoulder and took me to the door: 'Go back to earth and rest a little longer, my daughter, and try to be good so you won't stay so long in Purgatory.'

"That was my good dream, and that was how I finally knew I didn't have a son. I didn't learn it till very late, when my body was shrunk up and my spine was so bent I could hardly walk a step. Then the village began to empty out. Everybody went away and there wasn't any more charity for me to live on. I sat down to wait for death. After we found you my bones decided to rest. 'Nobody will even notice me,' I thought. I'm the kind that never disturbs anybody. And you see, I didn't even steal any space from the earth. They buried me in your grave, and I fit very well into the hollow of your arms. Only it occurs to me that I ought to be embracing you, not the other way around. Listen. It's raining up there. Can't you feel the raindrops falling?"

"It feels as if somebody were walking over us."

"You don't have to be afraid any more. They can't frighten you now. Just think about pleasant things, because we're going to be buried for a long time."

At daybreak, great drops of rain fell on the earth. They sounded hollow as they struck the soft loose dust of the furrows. A mockingbird flew level with the ground and imitated the wail of a baby. Farther on it uttered a groan as if of weariness, and still farther, where the horizon began to open out, it hiccuped and then laughed, and groaned again afterward.

Fulgor Sedano smelled the odor of the earth and looked out to see the rain staining the furrows. His little eyes were happy. He drank in three mouthfuls of that odor and smiled till his teeth showed.

"Good!" he said. "Another good year." And he added: "Keep at it, rain. Keep falling till you're all tired out. Then do the same over there. Remember, we've ploughed all the fields just to please you."

And he laughed.

The mockingbird that had flown over the fields came back and flew almost in front of him, and groaned again.

The rain was so heavy that the sky closed down, as if the night were returning.

The great gate of the Media Luna creaked as it opened. First two men rode out, then two more, then two more, till almost two hundred men on horseback had scattered out across the wet fields.

"Move the cattle at the Enmedio to beyond Estagua, and those at Estagua to the Vilmayo hills," Fulgor Sedano told them as they rode out. "And hurry up, the rains are here already."

He said it so many times that the last men out heard only, "From there to there, and from there to out there." They all raised their hands to their sombreros to show that they understood.

The last man had just left when Miguel Páramo came in at a gallop and swung down from his horse almost on top of Sedano. He let the horse look for its own stall.

"Where are you coming from so early, boy?"

"From milking."

"Who?"

"Can't you guess?"

"It must be Dorotea 'La Cuarraca.' She's the only one that's crazy about babies."

"You're an imbecile, Fulgor. But it isn't your fault."

And he walked away to eat breakfast, without even taking off his spurs.

In the kitchen, Damiana Cisneros asked him the same question: "But where have you come from, Miguel?"

"I've been out calling on mothers."

"Don't get cross. How do you want your eggs?"

"Any way you like them."

"I'm talking decently to you, Miguel."

"I know it, Damiana. Don't worry. But look, do you know somebody named Dorotea, the one they call 'La Cuarraca'?"

"Yes. If you want to see her, she's right outside. She comes here for her breakfast every morning. She carries a bundle around in her rebozo and croons to it. She says it's her baby. Something bad must have happened to her sometime, but she never talks about it so nobody knows what it was. She lives by begging."

"Damn that Fulgor! I'll teach him a lesson."

Then he began to wonder if the woman could be of some use to him. He went to the back door of the kitchen and called to her:

"Dorotea, come here. I want to make a deal with you."

When he came back in he was rubbing his hands.

"Where are those eggs?" he shouted to Damiana. "And from now on, give that woman the same things to eat you do me. And don't be stingy about it."

Fulgor Sedano went to the barn to check on the corn. He was worried about it, because it still wasn't harvest time. In fact, the fields had just been sown. "I want to see if we're going to run out." Then he added: "That boy! Exactly like his father, except that he's begun even sooner. At this rate he's sure to turn out bad. I forgot to tell him they came here yesterday to accuse him of killing somebody. If he keeps on like this . . ."

He sighed, and tried to imagine how far the horsemen had ridden, but he was distracted by Miguel Páramo's roan, which was rubbing its muzzle against the fence. "Didn't even unsaddle it," he thought. "And won't, either. Don Pedro's steadier, at least, and does some thinking now and then. But he spoils Miguel terribly. Yesterday when I told him what his son did, he said: 'Just consider that I did it, Fulgor. Miguel couldn't have done it, he isn't strong enough yet to kill anybody. To do that you have to have kidneys this big.' And he held his hands out as if he were measuring a pumpkin. 'Whatever he does, just say that I did it.'

"'Miguel's going to give you a lot of headaches, Don Pedro. He likes to quarrel.'

"'Let him be. He's just a child, Fulgor. How old is he? Seventeen, isn't he?'

"'Perhaps so. I remember when he was born. It seems like yesterday. But he's so violent. He lives in such a hurry, you'd think he was racing with time. I'm afraid he's going to end up bad.'

" 'He's just a baby, Fulgor.'

" 'Whatever you say, Don Pedro. But that woman who came here to say he killed her husband . . . I couldn't console her or make her stop crying. I know how to measure grief, Don Pedro, and she had it by the basketful. I offered her a hundred bushels of corn if she'd forget the affair, but she didn't want them. Then I promised her we'd make everything right in some way or other, but I just couldn't get her to be satisfied.'

" 'Who are they?'

" 'They're people I don't know.'

" 'Then there's nothing to worry about, Fulgor. Those people don't even exist.' "

When he entered the barn he could feel the warmth of the corn. He picked up a fistful of it to see if the weevils had got into it. Then he calculated how much was left.

"Good, it'll hold out," he said. "As soon as there's grass we won't need any corn for the cattle. We've got more than enough."

On the way back he looked up at the cloud-filled sky. "We're going to have rain for a good while." And he forgot about everything else.

"The seasons must be changing. My mother told me that when the rains begin, the air is full of light and the green smell of the new shoots. She told me how the clouds come on, how they spread out over the earth and change all its colors. . . . She lived the happiest part of her life here in this village, but she couldn't come back here to die. That's why she sent me in her place. It's strange, Dorotea, how I never even got to see the sky. But I suppose it must be the same one that she knew."

"I don't know, Juan Preciado. I didn't raise my head for so many years, I forgot all about the sky. And even if I'd looked up, what good would it have done? Heaven is a long way away, and my eyes were so blind that I was happy enough just to know where the ground was. Besides, I lost interest when Father Rentería told me I'd never go to Heaven, I'd never even see it from here. That was because of my sins. But he shouldn't have told me so. The only thing that gives life any meaning is the hope that when you die you'll go to a better place, and when they close that door to you and the only one that's left open is the door to Hell, then it's better not to have been born. For me, Juan Preciado, Heaven is right here where I am."

"And your soul? Where do you think it's gone?"

"It must be wandering around up there on earth, like all those others, looking for people to pray for it. I think it hates me for the bad things I did, but that doesn't worry me any more. I'm rid of all the pain it used to give me. It made me feel bitter about everything, even about not getting enough to eat, and it made the nights unbearable, full of terrifying thoughts. Visions of the damned and things like that. When I sat down to die, it told me to get up again and keep on living, as if it still hoped for some miracle that would clean away my sins. But I wouldn't. 'This is the end,' I told it. 'I can't go any farther.' I opened my mouth so it could leave, and it left. I felt something fall into my hands. It was the little thread of blood that had tied it to my heart."

They pounded at the door, but he didn't answer. He heard

them knock at all the doors, waking everybody up. He recognized Fulgor's steps as he hurried toward the great gate. They halted a moment, as if he intended to come back and knock again, and then went on.

He remembered the death of his father. It was also at daybreak, like this, except that on that morning the door was open, letting in the sad light of an ashen sky. And a woman leaned against the door, holding back her tears. The mother he had forgotten, had forgotten many times, saying to him, "They've killed your father."

He never wanted to revive the memory of that scene because it always brought on others, as if he had broken a full sack and was trying to keep the grain from spilling out. The death of his father reminded him of other deaths, and in each one of them there was the same image of a ruined face: one eye destroyed, the other with a vengeful glare. And another memory and another, until finally he erased it from his mind, when there wasn't anybody else who remembered.

"Put him down here. No, not like that. You have to put him in feet first. You! What are you waiting for?"

All in a low voice.

"And Don Pedro?"

"He's asleep. Don't wake him up. Don't make any noise."

But there he was, enormous in the doorway, staring at a bundle that had been wrapped up in old sacks as if in a shroud.

"Who is it?" he asked.

Fulgor Sedano came over to him. "It's Miguel, *patrón*."

"What have they done to him?" he shouted.

He expected to hear, 'They've killed him,' and he was holding back his anger as it swelled up within him, but he heard the soft voice of Fulgor Sedano saying, "Nobody did anything to him. He died by himself."

The light from the kerosene lamps was dim and yellow.

". . . The horse killed him," somebody said.

They laid him out on his bed, putting the mattress under it and setting him down on the plain boards. They crossed his hands on his breast and covered his face with a black cloth. "He looks bigger than he was," Fulgor Sedano whispered.

Pedro Páramo watched them without any expression on his face. His thoughts followed each other without connection, without meaning. At last he said: "I'm beginning to pay. It's better to pay early. You finish paying sooner."

He didn't feel any grief.

When he spoke to the people gathered in the patio, to thank them for coming, his voice cut through the wailing of the women, and afterwards the only sound was the stamping of Miguel Páramo's roan.

"Tell them to kill that animal," he said to Fulgor Sedano. "I don't want it to go on suffering."

"All right, Don Pedro. I understand. The poor creature must be grieving for him."

"That's just what I was thinking, Fulgor. And you might ask those women not to make such a racket. It's my corpse. They wouldn't howl like that if it were their own."

Many years later, Father Rentería still remembered the night when the hardness of his bed would not let him sleep and drove him outdoors. It was the night Miguel Páramo died.

He wandered through the solitary streets of Comala, his footsteps scaring the dogs that rooted in the garbage-heaps. When he came to the river he stopped there beside the calm water, watching the reflections of the stars that fell from heaven. He stayed for several hours, fighting with his thoughts, casting them into the black river.

"It all began," he thought, "when Pedro Páramo grew up and started taking over. His power grew like a weed. And the worst thing is, he got it from me. 'I want to confess that I slept with Pedro Páramo last night.' 'Father, I'm going to have a child by Pedro Páramo.' 'I loaned my daughter to Pedro Páramo, Father.' I always hoped he'd come to me to confess something, but he never did. He just extended his evil through that son of his. The one that he recognized, though God only knows why. All I know is that I put that instrument in his hands."

He recalled very clearly the day he brought Miguel to Pedro Páramo, newly born. He had said, "Don Pedro, the mother died in childbirth. She said you were the father. Here he is."

He didn't deny it, he merely said: "Why don't you keep him with you, Father? Make a priest out of him."

"I wouldn't want the responsibility. Not with the blood he's got in his veins."

"Do you really think he's got bad blood?"

"I do, Don Pedro."

"I'll prove to you you're wrong. Leave him here. There're plenty of people to take care of him."

"That's precisely what I was thinking. At least he won't lack food and clothing."

The baby was twisting like a snake, little as he was.

"Damiana! Take care of this. It's my son."

Then he opened a bottle. "Let's drink to the mother, and to you."

"And to the child?"

"To him, too. Why not?"

He poured another drink and they drank to the baby's future. That was what had happened.

The wagons began going by on the way to the Media Luna. He ducked down, hiding in the tall reeds that bordered the river. "Who are you hiding from?" he asked himself.

"Good morning, Father," he heard them call.

He stood up and answered, "Good morning, good morning. May God bless you."

The lights of the village were going out. The river was full of shining colors.

"Has the first bell rung yet?" one of the men asked him.

"It must have rung long ago," he replied, and walked off in the opposite direction so they would not detain him.

"Where are you going so early, Father?" "Who's dying, Father?" "Did somebody die in Contla, Father?"

He wanted to tell them: "I died. I'm the corpse." But he only smiled.

Beyond the village he walked faster. The sun was well up by the time he returned.

"Where have you been, Uncle?" Ana asked him. "A lot of the women came looking for you. They wanted to confess, because tomorrow's the first Friday."

"They can come back in the evening."

He sat silent for a little while on a bench in the entry, resting.

"How cool the air is, Ana!"

"No, it's hot, Uncle."

"It is?"

He was trying not to think about Contla. He had gone there to make a general confession to the priest, and the priest had denied him absolution.

"This man whose name you won't tell me has destroyed your church, and you've let him do it. What's left for you now? What have you done with the powers God gave you? I'd like to believe that you're a good priest and that everybody there thinks well of you, but mere goodness isn't enough. Sin isn't good, and to fight it you have to be hard and pitiless. I hope they're still faithful, but you're not protecting their faith, they keep it out of superstition and fear. I understand the poverty you live in, and I know how hard our task is in these poor villages. But that very fact gives me the right to tell you there's no need for us to give our blessings to certain people, because they pay you very little in exchange for your soul. And with your soul in their hands, how can you do your true work? No, my hands aren't clean enough to give you absolution. You'll have to ask for it somewhere else."

"Do you mean I should leave my church?"

"You'll have to. You can't keep on blessing others if you're in sin yourself."

"But what if they suspend me?"

"Perhaps you deserve it. That's for them to judge."

"But couldn't you. . . ? Provisionally, let's say. . . . I have to give extreme unction . . . Communion. So many people die in my village."

"Let God judge them."

"No, then?"

And the priest at Contla had told him no.

Afterwards they walked together along the shadowy verandas of the patio.   They sat down under an arbor on which grapes were ripening.

"They're bitter," the priest said, anticipating the question he was going to ask. "We live in a region where everything is given us, thanks to Providence, but where everything is bitter. That's what we're condemned to."

"You're right. I've tried to raise grapes in Comala. They don't bear. Only oranges and berries. Bitter oranges and bitter berries. I've forgotten what sweet things taste like. Do you remember the guavas we had at the seminary? And the peaches? And those tangerines? You just squeezed them a little and they popped out of their skins. I brought a few seeds here, not very many, just a little bagful. Afterwards I thought it would have been better to leave them back there where they grew, instead of bringing them here to die."

"Still, they say the land at Comala is good. It's a shame it's all in the hands of one man. Is Pedro Páramo still the owner?"

"That is God's will."

"I don't think God's will enters into this case. What do you think?"

"Sometimes I've had my doubts. But everybody there is sure of it."

"And you along with them?"

"I'm just a poor man, ready to humble himself . . . as long as he feels like doing so."

Then they said goodbye. He took the other priest's hands and kissed them. And now that he was here, back in reality, he didn't want to keep thinking of what happened in Contla.

He got up and went to the door.

"Where are you going, Uncle?"

His niece Ana was always there, always next to him, as if to shelter herself from life by hiding in his shadow.

"I'm going out for a little walk, Ana. It might help."

"Do you feel sick?"

"No, I'm not sick, Ana. I'm bad, I'm an evil man. That's what I feel."

He went to the Media Luna to offer his consolations to Pedro Páramo, and had to listen all over again to the excuses he made for his son. He let him talk. Nothing was important any more. He refused his invitation to eat with him: "I can't, Don Pedro, I have to be at the church early, because there's a whole crowd of women waiting for me to hear confession. Some other time."

He walked back and went directly to the church just as he was, dusty and miserable. He sat down to hear confession.

The first to come over was old Dorotea, who was always waiting there when he opened the doors of the church. She smelled of alcohol.

"So now you get drunk, do you? When did this start?"

"It's just that I went to Miguelito's wake, Father. And I drank too much. They gave me so much to drink, I made a clown of myself."

"You've never been anything else, Dorotea."

"But now I've sinned, Father. I've sinned a lot. More than enough."

He had told her on various occasions: "You never confess anything, Dorotea, you just come here to take up my time. You couldn't commit a sin now if you wanted to. Let the others confess."

"But this time it's true, Father."

"Tell me."

"Now that I can't do him any harm, I want to confess that I was the one that used to find girls for Miguelito."

Father Rentería thought for a little while, and then asked her, as if by habit: "Since when?"

"Since he was old enough. Since he first started to want them."

"Tell me again what you said, Dorotea."

"Why, that I was the one that got girls for Miguelito."

"Did you bring them to him?"

"Sometimes. Sometimes I just talked with them. And he just grabbed some of them himself. You know, when they were alone, when they didn't have anyone to help them."

"Were there many?"

He hadn't wanted to ask that question, but it slipped out.

"I even lost count, Father. An awful lot."

"What do you want me to say, Dorotea? Judge your own actions. See if you can pardon yourself."

"I can't, Father. But you can. That's why I came to see you."

"How many times have you come here begging me to send you to Heaven when you die? You want to go there to see if you can find your son, don't you? Well, now you can't go. But may God forgive you."

"Thank you, Father."

"And I forgive you, too, in His name. You can leave now."

"Aren't you going to give me any penance?"

"You don't need any, Dorotea."

"Thank you, Father."

"May God go with you."

He rapped with his knuckles on the little window of the

confession-box, to call another of the women over. When she began confessing, his head drooped as if he couldn't hold it up any longer. Then dizziness and confusion, he was drowning in dark waters, in spinning lights, the daylight was shattered to bits, there was a taste of blood on his tongue. While the voice droned on in his ear . . .

"All right, all right," he said. "How long has it been since you confessed?"

"Two days, Father."

And here she was again. It was as if he were surrounded with misery. "What are you doing here?" he asked himself. "Rest. Go and rest. You're too tired."

He left the confession-box and walked straight toward the sacristy. Without turning his head he said to the women who were waiting for him: "All those who feel they're without sin can receive the sacrament tomorrow."

There was only a low murmur behind him.

I'm lying on the bed where my mother died a long time ago. On the same mattress. With the same black wool blanket we slept under, mother and daughter. I used to sleep beside her then, in a little nest she made for me with her arms.

It's as if I could still feel the rhythm of her breathing, still hear her sighs . . . as if I could still feel the pain of her death.

But that's not true.

I'm here, face up, thinking about those days to forget my loneliness. Because I won't be lying here for only a little while. And I'm not in my mother's bed, I'm in a black box, like the coffins they use for burying the dead. Because I'm dead . . .

I remember where I am and I start thinking . . .

I think about that season of the year when the limes ripened. When the February wind bent down the fern shoots, before they dried up from neglect. When the ripe limes filled the patio with their fragrance.

The wind came down from the mountains on those February mornings. But the clouds stayed up above, waiting until it was time for them to enter the valley. They left the sky a blank blue. The sunlight shone down on the games the wind played as it made circles on the earth, stirring up the dust and shaking the boughs of the orange trees.

And the sparrows laughed. They pecked at the leaves the wind had blown down, and laughed. They chased the butterflies, and left a few feathers among the thorny branches, and laughed. It was that time of year.

February, when the mornings were wind and sparrows and blue light. I remember.

Then my mother died.

I should have cried out, I should have broken my hands by clasping them together in despair. That's what you wanted. But why couldn't it have been a happy morning? The wind came in through the open doors, rustling the morning-glory vine. The down had begun to grow on my legs, between the veins, and my hands were hot and trembling when they touched my forehead. The sparrows were playing. The wheat swayed on the hillsides. I was sorry that she couldn't see the wind playing in the jasmine, that she'd closed her eyes to the sunlight. But why should I have cried?

Do you remember, Justina? You set the chairs out along the

veranda so that the people who came to see her could wait their turn. They were empty. And my mother all alone among the candles. Her pale face. Her white teeth showing between her stiff purple lips. Her eyelids quiet now, and her heart too. And you and I together there, praying endless prayers without her hearing a word, without hearing anything ourselves, everything lost in the sound of the night wind.

You ironed her black dress, and you had starched the collar and the cuffs of the sleeves so that her hands would look right when we crossed them on her breast. On her old loving breast where I used to sleep. That fed me and cradled me.

Nobody came to see her. It was better that way. Death isn't handed out as if it were something good. Nobody goes looking for sorrow.

They knocked at the door. You answered it.

"You go," I said. "I don't want to see anybody. And tell them to go away. They want money for Gregorian Masses? But she didn't leave any money. She won't ever leave Purgatory if they don't sing those Masses? Who are they to judge, Justina? You say I'm crazy? All right."

The chairs stayed empty till we went out to bury her. Those hired men carried the coffin, sweating for a stranger's peso. They were strangers to our grief. They lowered the coffin into the tomb slowly and carefully, while the wind cooled them off after the long walk to the graveyard. Their eyes were cold, indifferent. They told you the price and you paid them as if you were shopping at the store. You'd wet your handkerchief and wrung it out again and again, and now you untied it and took out the funeral money . . .

After they went away you knelt down on her grave and kissed

the earth, and you might have started digging if I hadn't said: "Let's go home, Justina. She isn't here. There's nothing here except a dead body."

"Was it you that said all that, Dorotea?"

"What? I was napping for a while. Are they still frightening you?"

"I heard somebody talking. A woman's voice. I thought it was you."

"A woman's voice? It must be the one that talks to herself. Doña Susanita. She's buried in the big tomb near us. The dampness must have reached her and she's turning in her sleep."

"Who is she?"

"Pedro Páramo's last wife. Some people say she's crazy, some say she isn't. The truth is, she talked to herself even when she was alive."

"She must have died a long time ago."

"Oh, yes. Long ago. What did you hear her say?"

"Something about her mother."

"But she didn't even have a mother."

"Well, that's what she talked about."

"At least, she didn't bring her here when she came. No, wait, I remember now. She was born here, and yes, her mother died of consumption. Her mother was a strange woman, she never visited anybody."

"That's what she was saying, that nobody went to see her mother when she died."

"But what times would she be remembering? Of course people wouldn't go into the house, they were afraid of catching consumption. Does she remember all that?"

"Yes, that's what she was talking about."

"Next time you hear her, let me know. I'd like to hear what she says."

"Listen. I think she's going to say something. I can hear a murmur."

"No, that's not her. It's farther away, from over in the other direction. And it's a man's voice. What happens to these old corpses is that when the dampness reaches them they begin to stir. And then they wake up. Listen, he's speaking."

". . . Heaven is great. God was with me that night. If He hadn't been I don't know what would have happened. Because it was already dark when I came to again . . ."

"Can you hear him, Juan Preciado?"

"Yes."

". . . I had blood all over me. When I got up, my hands splashed in a pool of blood on the stones. And it was mine. A lake of blood. But I wasn't dead. I could tell. I knew that Don Pedro didn't intend to kill me. Just to scare me, that's all. He wanted to find out if I'd been in Vilmayo two months before. On the day of San Cristóbal. At the wedding. What wedding? Which day? I splashed in my own blood and asked him, 'What wedding, Don Pedro? No, no, Don Pedro, I wasn't there. Maybe I went by the place that day, but it was just by pure chance . . .' He didn't intend to kill me. He left me a cripple, as you can see. But he didn't kill me. They say that one of my eyes was crossed from then on, from the scare he gave me. The fact is, I was more of a man afterwards. Heaven is great. Nobody can doubt that . . ."

"Who is he, Dorotea?"

"One of a whole crowd. Pedro Páramo caused such a slaughter after his father was shot, they say he killed off almost everybody who was at the wedding. Don Lucas Páramo was going to be best man, but what happened was just an accident, because it was the bridegroom they wanted to kill. Pedro Páramo couldn't find out who fired the bullet, so he took his revenge on everybody. The wedding was out there in the Vilmayo hills, where there used to be some ranches that disappeared a long time ago. . . . Listen, I think she's talking again. You've got young ears, pay attention, so you can tell me what she says."

"I can't understand her. I don't think she's talking, just moaning."

"About what?"

"I don't know."

"It must be about something. She wouldn't moan for nothing. Listen harder."

"She's only moaning, that's all. Perhaps Pedro Páramo made her suffer."

"Don't you believe it. I can tell you he never loved any other woman the way he loved her. He loved her so much that he spent the rest of his life hunched over in a chair, looking at the road where they took her out to bury her. He lost interest in everything. He let the fields stay empty, and had all the equipment burned. Some people say it was because he was tired, and others because he was disillusioned, but the one sure thing is that he sent everybody away and just sat there in his chair, with his face to the road.

"After that the fields all went to ruin. It was a pity to see them choking up with weeds and scrub from not being ploughed. That was when people began to leave. The men went first, to look for other work. I can remember days when Comala was full of goodbyes, and it even seemed a happy thing to say goodbye to those that were leaving. They meant to come back, so they left their families and things behind. Then some of them sent for their families, though not for their belongings, and after that they seemed to forget all about the village and the rest of us, even about their things. I stayed on because I didn't have anywhere to go. Others stayed and waited for Pedro Páramo to die, because they said he'd promised to will them his property, and they kept on living here with that hope. But years and years went by and he didn't die, he just sat there in the Media Luna like a scarecrow.

"Not long before he died the Cristeros revolted and the troops took away the few men that were left here. That was when I began to die of hunger, and I never caught up.

"And all that because of Don Pedro's ideas. Because of his grief. Just because his wife died, that Susanita. So you can imagine whether he loved her."

Fulgor Sedano asked him, "Do you know who came back, *patrón*?"

"Who?"

"Bartolomé San Juan."

"So?"

"That's exactly what I asked myself: What's he doing here?"

"You haven't investigated?"

"No. The thing is that he hasn't looked for a house. He went straight to the old house you used to live in. He dismounted and took down his saddlebags just as if you'd already rented the place to him. At least that's how it looked."

"What's the matter with you, Fulgor? You're supposed to find out what goes on. Isn't that what you're for?"

"I got fooled a little. But I'll investigate tomorrow, if you think it's necessary."

"Leave tomorrow to me. I'll take care of them. Did they both come back?"

"Yes, he and his wife. How did you know?"

"It wouldn't be his daughter?"

"From the way he treats her I'd say she's his wife."

"You can go to bed, Fulgor."

"Good night, Don Pedro."

"I've waited thirty years for you to come back, Susana," Pedro Páramo said. "I hoped to have everything. Not just something: everything. Everything we could possibly want . . . and all of it for you. How many times did I invite your father to live here again? I told him I needed him. I even told him things that weren't true.

"I offered him the job of foreman, just to see you again. And how did he reply? 'No answer,' the messenger always said. 'Don Bartolomé tears up your letters when I deliver them.' But I learned from the messenger that you had married, and then that you were a widow and lived with your father again.

"Then the silence. The messenger came and went, and every time he returned he told me: 'I couldn't find them, Don Pedro. I was told they left Mascota. But nobody could agree about where they went.'

"And I said: 'Don't worry about expenses. Find them. Even if the earth has swallowed them up.'

"Finally he came back one day and told me: 'I've searched the whole sierra trying to find out where Don Bartolomé San

Juan is hiding, and at last I've discovered him. He's out there in a hole in the mountains, living in a log shelter near the abandoned mines they call La Andrómeda.'

"There were strange winds blowing in those days. It was said that a revolution had broken out. We heard rumors of it. That was what brought your father here. Not for himself, he said in his letter, but for your safety. He wanted to bring you to a place where there were people.

"I felt as if Heaven had opened. I wanted to run to you. To surround you with happiness. To cry. And I did cry, Susana, when I knew you were coming back."

"Some villages taste of bad luck. You can tell them by drinking a little of their stale air. It's poor and thin, like everything else that's old. This is one of those villages, Susana.

"Back at La Andrómeda you could at least pass the time watching things being born: the clouds, the birds, the moss. Do you remember? But there isn't anything here except that stale yellow smell wherever you go. The village is bad luck. Nothing but bad luck.

"He asked us to come back. He's loaned us his house, and given us everything we need. But we don't have to be grateful to him. It's a misfortune that we're here, because we're not going to have any luck. I can tell.

"Do you know what Pedro Páramo told me? I didn't expect that what he gave us was free, and I was ready to pay him back by working, since we'd have to pay him somehow. I told him all about La Andrómeda, and made him see it had possibilities if it were worked correctly. And do you know what he said? 'I'm not interested in the mine, Bartolomé San Juan. The only thing I want from you is your daughter. She's the best work you've ever done.'

"He loves you, Susana. He says that you played with him when you were both little. That he knows you. That when you were little you went swimming together in the river. I didn't know that. If I had, I would have beaten you to death."

"I don't doubt it."

"Did you say that to me? That you don't doubt it?"

"Yes, I said it."

"You mean you want to sleep with him?"

"Yes, Bartolomé."

"Don't you know he's married? Don't you know he's had hundreds of women?"

"Yes, Bartolomé."

"Don't call me Bartolomé! I'm your father!"

Bartolomé San Juan, a dead miner. Susana San Juan, the daughter of a miner dead in the mines of La Andrómeda. He saw it clearly: "I'll have to go there to die," he thought. Then he said:

"You're a widow, but I told him that you're still living with your husband, or that at least you act that way. I've tried to talk him out of his idea, but he just squints at me when I talk to him, and when I mention your name he shuts his eyes. I know what that means. That's sheer evil. That's Pedro Páramo."

"And who am I?"

"You're my daughter. Mine. The daughter of Bartolomé San Juan."

The thoughts began to stir in Susana's mind, slowly at first, then racing so fast that she could only say: "It isn't true. It isn't true."

"Why does the world press in on us from all sides, and break us into pieces, and water the ground with our blood? What have we done? Why have our souls rotted? Your mother said that at least God's charity would be left to us. And you deny it, Susana. Why do you say I'm not your father? Are you insane?"

"Didn't you know?"

"Are you insane?"

"Of course I am, Bartolomé. Didn't you know?"

"Do you know, Fulgor, she's the most beautiful woman in the world. I thought I'd lost her forever. And now I don't want to lose her again. Do you understand, Fulgor? Tell her father to keep on working the mines. And out there . . . I imagine it would be very easy for the old man to vanish out there. Nobody ever goes there. Isn't that right?"

"It could be."

"It has to be. She has to be left an orphan. And it's our obligation to take care of orphans and such. Right?"

"It doesn't sound too difficult."

"Then get to work, Fulgor, get to work."

"But what if she finds out?"

"Who's going to tell her? Look, between the two of us, who's going to tell her?"

"I don't think anybody is."

"Never mind your 'I don't think.' You'll see, everything will

work out. Remind him of what he wanted to do at La Andrómeda. Send him back out there to work, but tell him not to live
out there. And tell him not to cart his daughter along when he
goes, because we'll take care of her here. He'll have his work
out there and his home back here. Put it like that, Fulgor."

"I like the way you're planning this, *patrón*. It's as if you were
a young man all over again."

Rain was falling on the fields in the Comala valley. It was
a light rain, unusual in a region that only knows cloudbursts.
It was Sunday, and the Indians had come down from Apango
with their strings of little fruit, their rosemary, their bunches of
thyme. They had not brought any ocote because the wood was
damp, nor any leafmold either because that was damp also
from the long rain. They spread out their herbs under the arcade
and waited.

The rain went on falling on the puddles. The water ran in
rivers along the furrows where the new corn was sprouting. The
men could not come to the market because they were breaking
the furrows so that the water would run in other courses and
not wash out the new shoots. They worked in groups, slogging
across the flooded fields in the rain, breaking up the soft clods
with their shovels, firming the shoots with their hands and trying
to protect them so that they would grow tall and strong.

The Indians waited. They felt it was an unlucky day. Perhaps
that is why they shivered in their straw raincapes, not from the
cold but from fear. They watched the rain falling, and stared
up at the clouded sky.

Nobody came. The village appeared deserted. By the middle of the day their capes were heavy with dampness. They gossiped, they told jokes and laughed at them. The strings of fruit glistened with drops of moisture. "If we had just brought a little pulque," they thought, "it wouldn't matter about the rain. But the maguey fields were a sea of mud, so what could we do?"

Justina Díaz came down the street that led in from the Media Luna, dodging the streams that spurted onto the sidewalk from the roof drains. She crossed herself as she passed the gate to the church, and went into the arcade. The Indians all turned to look at her. It was as if they were searching her with their eyes. She stopped at the first display, bought ten centavos' worth of rosemary, and turned away, followed by those silent looks.

"Everything's so expensive nowadays," she said to herself as she walked back to the Media Luna. "Ten centavos for this pitiful little bunch of rosemary. There isn't even enough of it to have any odor."

The Indians packed up their wares at dusk, and stepped out into the rain with their heavy bundles on their shoulders. They went to the church to pray to the Virgin, and left her a bunch of thyme as an offering. Then they set out for Apango. As they walked along they told jokes and laughed at them.

Justina Díaz went into Susana San Juan's bedroom and put the bunch of rosemary on the wall bracket. The drawn curtains shut out the light, so that all she could see were the black shadows. She supposed that Susana San Juan was asleep. She wished that she would always stay asleep. But then she heard a faint sigh, that seemed to come out of a dark corner of the room.

"Justina."

She turned her head. She couldn't see anybody, but she felt his hand on her shoulder, and then his breath in her ear. He whispered: "Go away, Justina. Pack your things and go. We don't need you any more."

"She needs me," she said, straightening up. "She's sick and she needs me."

"Not any more, Justina. I'm going to stay here and take care of her."

"Is that you, Don Bartolomé?" And her scream was so loud that even the men and women coming back from the fields could hear it. They said: "It sounded human. But who ever heard a human being scream like that?"

The rain was turning to hail, muffling all sounds except its own.

"What happened, Justina? Why did you scream?"

"I didn't scream. You must have been dreaming, Susana."

"I've already told you I never dream. You don't have any consideration for me. I'm dreadfully tired. Last night you didn't put the cat out and it wouldn't let me sleep."

"It slept with me, between my legs. It was soaking wet and I felt sorry for it, so I let it sleep in my bed. But it didn't make any noise."

"No, no noise. It just had a circus jumping from my feet to my head and back again, and mewing for something to eat."

"I fed it in the evening and it never left me all night. You're dreaming things again, Susana."

"I tell you it spent the whole night scaring me with its jumping around. Your cat is very affectionate, but I don't want it in here when I'm trying to sleep."

"You're seeing visions, Susana, that's what's the matter. When Pedro Páramo comes I'm going to tell him I can't put up with you any longer. I'm going to tell him I'm leaving. There's plenty of good people who'll give me work. They aren't maniacs like you, always making trouble. I'm leaving tomorrow and I'll take my cat with me and then you can sleep."

"You're a wicked woman, Justina, but you won't go away. You won't go anywhere, because you know you can't find anybody who loves you the way I do."

"No, I won't go away, Susana. I'm here to take care of you. It doesn't matter what you do, I'll still be here."

She had taken care of her ever since she was born. She had held her in her arms, had taught her to walk, had seen her grow. She had looked into her eyes, those eyes that resembled candy. "Mint candy is blue. Yellow and blue. Green and blue. Mint and wintergreen together." She had nipped her legs, and amused her by giving her her breasts, although they were dry and only served as toys. "Look," she told her, "play with this, it's a toy." She had hugged and squeezed her.

The rain pattered on the banana leaves. It sounded as if the raindrops were boiling in the water that stood on the earth.

The sheets were cold and damp. The drains gushed and foamed, working all day, all night, all day. The water ran and ran, hissing with a million bubbles.

It was midnight, and the noise of the rain hushed all other sounds.

Susana San Juan sat up and got out of bed. She felt that

strange heaviness again, weighing down her feet, moving around the edges of her body, trying to find her face.

"Is that you, Bartolomé?"

She thought she heard the door creak, as if somebody had come in or gone out. And then only the cold rain falling on the banana leaves.

She went back to sleep, and didn't wake up till there was light on the red bricks of the floor. The bricks were sprinkled with dew. It was the gray morning of a new day.

"Justina!" she cried.

And Justina appeared at once, wrapping herself up in a blanket. "What do you want, Susana?"

"It's that cat. It got in again."

"My poor Susana!"

She lay on her breast, embracing her, until she raised her head and asked: "Why are you crying, Justina? I'll tell Pedro Páramo you're very good to me. I won't say a word about the way your cat frightens me. Please don't cry, Justina."

"Your father's dead, Susana. He died the night before last, and they came here today to tell us they've already buried him. They couldn't bring him here because it's too far. You're all alone now, Susana."

"So it *was* my father." She smiled. "He came here to say good-bye to me," she said, and smiled.

Many years before, when she was still a little girl, he had said to her: "Lower, Susana, and tell me what you see."

She was hanging from a rope. It hurt her waist and made her

hands bleed, but she didn't want to get loose because it was the only thread that joined her with the world outside.

"I don't see anything, papá."

"Look harder, Susana. There has to be something."

And he lighted her with his lamp.

"I don't see anything, Papá."

"I'll let you down farther. Tell me when you're at the bottom."

She had entered through a little hole among the slabs, and had groped across the old rotten planks, all splintered and covered with dust.

"Lower, Susana. You'll find what I told you."

And she went down and down, swaying and rocking in the darkness, with her feet searching for a hold.

"Lower, Susana, lower. Tell me if you see anything."

When she reached the bottom she stood still, too frightened to speak. The beam of the lamp circled around until it found her. She trembled at her father's shout:

"Bring me up what's down there, Susana!"

She picked up the skull, and when she saw it in the light she dropped it.

"It's a skull," she said.

"Bring me everything you find. There ought to be something else near it."

The skull crumbled into fragments. The jawbone came loose as if it were made of sugar. She gathered piece after piece until she reached the little bones of the toes.

"Look for something more, Susana. Money. Round wheels of gold. Look for them, Susana."

She didn't know about her then, not until many days later, while she was suffering from the icy looks of her father.

That's why she was laughing now.

"I was sure it was you, Bartolomé."

And poor Justina, who was weeping on her breast, had to get up when she saw she was laughing. Then the laugh changed to a wild cackle.

It was still raining. The Indians had gone. It was Monday, and the Comala valley was still drowned in the rain.

The wind blew during all those days, the wind that brought the rain. The rain had gone now, but the wind stayed on. The corn-shoots dried off in the fields and lay down to protect themselves from the wind. It was bearable enough in the daytime, although it shook the vines and rattled the tiles on the roof, but at night it moaned and moaned. The clouds drifted like great silent pavilions over the earth.

Susana San Juan heard the gale pounding at the closed window. She was lying with her hands behind her head, thinking, listening to the sounds of the night. It was as if the night were being dragged back and forth by the restless breath of the wind.

The door opened. A puff of air blew out the lamp. She saw the darkness and stopped her thoughts. She heard little murmurs, then the uneven beating of her heart. She half glimpsed the flame when its light fell on her closed eyelids.

She didn't open her eyes. Her hair was spread over her face. The light brought drops of sweat to her lips. She asked: "Is that you, Father?"

"It is, my daughter."

She half opened her eyes. Through her tangled hair she could see a great shadow on the ceiling. And through her wet lashes, a dark figure in front of her. A vague light. A light where the heart is, in the form of a small heart that pulsed like a wavering flame. "Your heart is dying of grief," she thought. "You've come here to tell me that Florencio is dead, but I already know. Don't worry about me. I've got my sorrow put away in a safe place. Don't let your heart burn out."

She got up and dragged herself to where Father Rentería was standing.

"Let me try to console you a little," he said, sheltering the flame of the candle with his hands.

Father Rentería let her come up to him. He watched her circle the flame with her hands and then bend her face down to the wick, until the smell of burning flesh made him blow it out.

The darkness returned and she ran to hide under the sheets.

Father Rentería said, "I've come to comfort you, my daughter."

"Then goodbye, Father," she answered, "don't come back. I don't need you."

She heard the footsteps going away, the footsteps that always made her feel cold, cold and trembling and afraid.

"Why do you come to see me if you're dead?"

Father Rentería closed the door and walked out into the night. The wind was still blowing.

A man they called El Tartamudo arrived at the Media Luna and asked for Pedro Páramo.

"Why do you want to see him?"

"I want to t-talk with him."

"He isn't here."

"When he comes b-back, tell him it's about D-don Fulgor."

"I'll go look for him, but it might take hours."

"T-tell him it's important."

The man called El Tartamudo waited on his horse. In a little while Pedro Páramo came over to him.

"What do you want?"

"I have to talk d-directly with the *p-patrón*."

"I'm the *patrón*. What's your business?"

"Just this. They killed Don Fulgor S-sedano. I was with him. We went out to see how much water was in the ditches. We s-saw a lot of men coming out to m-meet us, and one of them said, 'I know who he is. He's the f-foreman of the Media Luna.'

"They didn't pay any attention to m-me, but they told Don Fulgor to get off his horse. They t-told him they were revolutionaries. They said they w-wanted your lands. 'Start running,' they told Don Fulgor. 'G-go tell your *patrón* we'll be seeing him.' And he started r-running. Not very fast, because he was so heavy, but the b-best he could. And they shot him while he was running. He d-died with one foot on the ground and one in the air.

"I d-didn't even move. I waited till it was dark, and then I c-came here to tell you what happened."

"Well, what are you waiting for? Why don't you get going. Tell them I'm right here if they have any business with me. But first go over to La Consagración. Do you know El Tilcuate? He'll be there. Tell him I have to see him. And tell those men I'll be waiting for them whenever they have time. What kind of revolutionaries are they?"

"I d-don't know. They just said that that's what they're called."

"Tell El Tilcuate I need him here at once."

"G-good, *patrón*."

Pedro Páramo shut himself into his office again. He felt old and worn out. He didn't care about Fulgor, who had already served his purpose. Though he was very useful at times. "Anyway," he thought, "El Tilcuate will take care of those idiots."

He thought of Susana San Juan, always in her room, asleep, or if not sleeping, then as if she were. He had spent all last night leaning against the wall, staring at her by the faint light of the votive candle. Staring at her restive body. At her sweating face. At her hands as they toyed with the sheets, as they clawed the pillow.

Since he brought her here to live, the nights he spent at her side had all been like that, unhappy, endlessly disturbing. He asked himself when it would end.

Someday, he hoped, someday. Nothing can last forever. There isn't any memory, no matter how intense, that doesn't fade out at last.

If only he could discover what made her toss and turn in her sleep, as if something were destroying her from within. . . . But even if she were herself again, would it be enough for her to know that she was the creature he loved best in all the world? And to know also, and this was more important, that she would help him depart from this world drunk with the image that erased all other memories?

But which world was Susana San Juan living in? That was one of the things that Pedro Páramo never found out.

"My body loved to stretch itself out on the hot sand. I closed my eyes and spread my arms and legs to the soft breeze that

came in from the sea. And the sea came up and washed my feet
with its foam . . ."

"That's the one that talks, Juan Preciado. Don't forget to tell
me what she says."

". . . It was still early. The waves rose and fell. They left their
foam on the beach and changed into green ripples.

"'I like to bathe in the sea naked,' I told him. That's why he
followed me that first day. He was naked too, and he glowed
when he came out of the water. There weren't any seagulls, only
those birds that sound as if they're snoring. They disappear after
the sun comes up. He followed me that first day, but he felt
lonely, even though I was there with him.

"'You're just like one of those birds,' he said. 'I like you better
at night when we're together in the darkness, under the same
sheet, with our heads on the same pillow . . .'

"And he left.

"I went back to the sea. I always went back. And the sea
washed my ankles, my knees and thighs. It clasped its gentle
arms around my waist. It stroked my forehead, and kissed my
throat, and hugged my shoulders. I hid myself in it, in its
strength and gentleness . . .

"'I like to bathe in the sea,' I told him.

"But he didn't understand.

"And the next morning I was out on the beach again, to clean
myself. To give myself up to the sea . . ."

The men arrived at dusk, about twenty of them, all carrying
arms.

Pedro Páramo invited them to supper. They sat down at the table without taking off their sombreros, and without saying a word. The only sound they made was when they drank their cups of chocolate or ate their tortillas and beans.

Pedro Páramo watched them. He didn't recognize a single face. El Tilcuate stood behind him in the shadows.

"Gentlemen," he said when he saw they had finished eating, "what else can I do for you?"

"Are you the owner here?" one of them asked with a wave of his hand.

But another one interrupted him: "I'll do the talking."

"Good," Pedro Páramo said. "But what can I do for you?"

"As you see, we've taken up arms."

"And?"

"That's all. Isn't that enough?"

"But why have you done it?"

"Because a lot of others have done the same thing. Didn't you know about it? We're waiting till we get instructions, and then we'll know what it's all about. For the time being, we're here."

"I know what it's about," another one said, "and if you'd like, I'll tell you. We've rebelled against the government and against people like you because we're sick of putting up with you. Because the government is rotten and because you and your kind are just stupid crooks and bandits. I won't say any more about the government because we're going to do our talking with bullets."

"How much do you need for your revolution?" Pedro Páramo asked. "Maybe I can help you."

"The man's all right, Perseverancio. You ought to keep your

mouth shut. We need a rich man to back us, so why not this gentleman here? Look, Casildo, about how much do we need?"

"Let him give us as much as he wants to."

"That's no good. What do you think we're here for? We should take everything he's got, including the corn he's got stuffed in his belly."

"Calm down, Perseverancio. We don't want to make trouble if we don't have to. Let's reach an agreement. You do the talking, Casildo."

"Well, I figure that about twenty thousand pesos wouldn't be too bad for a beginning. What do the rest of you think? Perhaps this gentleman here will even think it's too little, since he's offered to help us out of his own free will. Let's say fifty thousand, then. All right?"

"I'm going to give you a hundred thousand pesos," Pedro Páramo told them. "How many men have you got?"

"About three hundred."

"Good. I'll lend you another three hundred to strengthen your group. I'll have the men and the money all ready for you within a week. The money is a gift from me, but the men are only loaned, so send them back here when you're through with them. Is that all right?"

"Of course."

"Then a week from now, gentlemen. And it's been a pleasure knowing you."

The last man to leave said: "But just remember that if you don't do what you've promised, you'll be hearing from Perseverancio. That's my name."

Pedro Páramo shook his hand and wished him good night.

"Which one of them do you think is the leader?" he asked
El Tilcuate.

"Well, I have an idea it's the fat one that was in the middle
and didn't even raise his eyes. I've got a hunch that he is. I'm
not wrong very often, Don Pedro."

"No, Damasio, you're the leader. Or don't you want to join
the revolution?"

"Of course I do. The sooner the better."

"Good. You don't need any advice from me. Get together three
hundred men you can trust and join up with those frauds. Tell
them you've brought the men I promised. You know how to take
care of the rest yourself."

"What about the money? Will I bring that along too?"

"I'm going to give you ten pesos for each man, just for their
most urgent expenses. Tell them I'll keep the rest of it here for
them. It wouldn't be convenient for them to carry it around.
By the way, how do you like that little ranch they call Puerta
de Piedra? Good, then, it's yours from right now. I'll give you
a message to Gerardo Trujillo, the lawyer in Comala, and he'll
put the property in your name. What do you say, Damasio?"

"You don't have to ask, *patrón*. Although I'd do the same job
with or without the ranch, just for the pleasure of it. It's as
if you didn't even know me. But I appreciate it all the same.
My wife will at least be able to support herself while I'm gone."

"And look, drive some of my cows out there. The ranch isn't
any good without any stock on it."

"Is it all right if they're Brahmans?"

"Pick out any you want, as many as you think your woman
can take care of. But getting back to business, make sure you

don't go too far away from my lands, so that if others arrive
they'll see we've already got troops here. And come see me when
you can, or when you have news."

"I will, *patrón*."

"What is she saying, Juan Preciado?"

"She says she used to put her feet between his legs. Her feet
were cold as stones, and she'd warm them like that till they
were like bread baking in an oven. He'd bite her feet and tell
her they were like new-baked bread. She used to sleep all nestled
up in him, hiding herself within him. She says she used to feel
lost in a dark nothingness when she felt her flesh being broken
open like a furrow being opened by a burning spike. Then it
wasn't burning, it was warm and sweet, striking hard blows
against her soft flesh. She felt she was sinking, was being swallowed up, and she moaned. But his death hurt her worse.
That's what she says."

"Who is she talking about?"

"Somebody who must have died before she did."

"Yes, but who?"

"I don't know. She says that the night he was so late in coming
back, she sensed that he came in very late, maybe at dawn. She
hardly noticed, though, because of her feet. They'd been cold
before that, but then they seemed to be wrapped up in something, as if somebody had come in and put something around
them so they'd be warm. When she woke up she found they
were wrapped in a newspaper. She'd been reading it while she
waited for him, and let it fall on the floor when she couldn't

stay awake any longer. It was still around her feet when they came to tell her he was dead."

"I think her coffin must have broken. I can hear the boards squeaking."

"Yes, I can hear them too."

That night she dreamed again. Why did she have to remember so many things, and so passionately? Why not just remember his death, and not all that tender music of the past?

"Florencio is dead, señora."

How tall he was! Tall and straight. With a hard voice, as dry as the driest earth, and a heavy body . . . or did it get heavy afterwards? "What did they tell me? Florencio? Which Florencio? Mine? Oh, why didn't I weep, why didn't I drown myself in tears to wash away my grief? You don't exist, God! I begged You to protect him. To take care of him. But You don't care about anything except our souls. And what I want is his body. Naked . . . hot with love . . . boiling with desire. Pressed against my trembling bosom and arms. My transparent body suspended from his, sustained by his strength. And what will I do with my lips now, without his mouth to kiss them? What will I do with my poor lips?"

Pedro Páramo stood near the door, watching her twist and gesture, counting the long minutes of this new dream. The lamp sputtered and the flame grew weaker and weaker and then went out.

If only she were suffering from grief, and not these endless, exhausting dreams, he could try to find her some consolation for it. That is what Pedro Páramo was thinking as he watched her, as he followed her slightest motion. What would have happened if she had died when the flame died?

Later he went away, closing the door silently behind him. The clean night air freed him of her image.

She woke up a little before dawn, soaked with sweat. She threw the heavy covers onto the floor, then the sheet too. Her body lay naked in the cool wind of daybreak. She sighed and went back to sleep.

That is how Father Rentería found her, hours later: naked and fast asleep.

"Did you know they defeated El Tilcuate, Don Pedro?"

"I know there was a lot of shooting last night, because I could hear the racket. But that's all. Who told you, Gerardo?"

"Some of the wounded came back to Comala, and my wife helped to bandage them. They told her they were Damasio's men. They said a lot of them had been killed. It seems they were fighting against the troops of somebody named Villa."

"I don't know, Gerardo, it looks as if we're going to see bad times. What are you planning to do?"

"I'm going away, Don Pedro. To Sayula. I'll open up an office there and start over."

"I envy you lawyers. You can go anywhere you want, without worrying about your lands or anything."

"Don't you believe it. We have our own problems. Besides, it's hard to say goodbye to people like yourself, and I appreciate all the favors you've done me. Where do you want me to leave the papers?"

"Don't leave them, take them with you. Or can't you handle my affairs from there?"

"I'm grateful for your confidence, Don Pedro. I'm sincerely grateful. But I'm afraid it would be impossible. Certain . . . let's say . . . irregularities. . . . Things that nobody except you ought to know about. It would be very dangerous if the papers got into the wrong hands. It's much safer to keep them here with you."

"You're right, Gerardo. Leave them here and I'll burn them. With papers or without them, who can argue with me about what I own?"

"Nobody, Don Pedro. Absolutely nobody. Excuse me now."

"Go with God, Gerardo."

"What did you say?"

"I said, may God be with you."

The lawyer Gerardo Trujillo walked out slowly. He was old now, but not so old as to take such little shuffling steps. The truth was that he was hoping for a gift. He had served Don Lucas, Don Pedro's father, may he rest in peace, and then Don Pedro, and Don Pedro's son Miguel, and he was hoping for a gift. For a large gift. He had told his wife:

"I'm going to say goodbye to Don Pedro. I'm sure he'll reward me for all I've done for him. We can get established in Sayula with the money, and live comfortably the rest of our lives."

But why do women always have doubts? Do they get information from Heaven, or what?

"No," she said, "you're going to work just as hard in Sayula, because you won't get anything here."

"What makes you say that?"

"I just know."

He walked toward the door, ready to be called back: "Say, Gerardo! I've been so busy I haven't had a chance to think about you. But I owe you favors that can't be paid with money. Please take this, it's a small gift, a token."

But the call never came. He walked out the door and untied his horse, then climbed into the saddle and rode slowly toward Comala, all the while hoping to be called back. When he saw that the Media Luna was far behind him, he thought: "I'd have lowered myself if I'd asked him for a loan."

"Don Pedro, I've come back, because I'm not satisfied with what I said. I'd like to keep on handling your affairs."

He was sitting in Don Pedro's office again, only half an hour after he left it.

"Good, Gerardo. The papers are right there where you put them."

"I'd also like . . . the expenses . . . you know . . . something in advance . . . something extra, if it's all right with you."

"Five hundred?"

"Couldn't it be a little more. Just a little more?"

"Will you be satisfied with a thousand?"

"What about five?"

"Five what? Five thousand pesos? I don't have that much. You know that everything's invested in land and stock. Take a thousand. I'm sure you don't need more."

He sat there thinking, with his head bowed. He heard the pesos clinking onto the desk where Pedro Páramo was counting out the money. He thought of Don Lucas, who had died owing him certain fees. Of Don Pedro, who started a new account. Of his son Miguel. How that boy used to embarrass him! He must have got him out of jail at least fifteen times, maybe more. And then the time he murdered . . . what was his name? Rentería, that's it. They had to put a pistol in his hand after he was dead. Miguelito was badly frightened, even though he used to laugh about it afterwards. Now what would it have cost Don Pedro if these things had gotten to the authorities? And what about the women? How many times did he have to take money out of his own pocket so that they'd keep quiet? "You ought to be glad your baby'll have light skin," he told them.

"Here you are, Gerardo. Take good care of them, because they don't come back."

He was still deep in his thoughts, and replied:

"No. Neither do the dead." Then he added: "Unfortunately."

It was an hour or two before daybreak. The sky was crowded with fat, swollen stars. The moon had come out for a little while and then vanished. It was one of those sad moons that nobody looks at or even notices. It hung there for a little while, pale and disfigured, and then hid itself behind the mountains.

The bulls were lowing far off in the darkness.

"Those animals never sleep," Damiana Cisneros said. "Never. They're like the devil himself, who's always looking for souls to take down to Hell."

She turned over in bed, with her face near the wall.

Then she heard the knocking.

She held her breath and opened her eyes. She heard it again, three sharp knocks, as if somebody were rapping at the wall with his knuckles. Not here, opposite her. Farther away. But on the same wall.

"God save me! That's the way San Pascual Bailón always knocks, three times, when he comes to tell one of his followers that the hour of his death has arrived."

And since she hadn't been to the church to pray to him for a long time, on account of her rheumatism, she wasn't too worried. But she was frightened by the sound, and more than frightened, curious.

She got out of bed without making any noise and peered out of the window.

Everything was in darkness, but she knew the place so well that she could make out the huge form of Pedro Páramo climbing into Margarita's window.

"Ah, that Don Pedro!" Damiana said. "Still the tomcat! But I don't understand why he has to do everything in secret. If he'd just let me know, I'd have told Margarita that the *patrón* needed her tonight, and he wouldn't even have had the bother of getting out of bed."

Later she had to take off her nightgown, because the night was growing hot . . .

"Damiana!"

That had been in the days when she was still a young girl.

"Damiana, open the door!"

Her heart trembled as if it were a toad jumping behind her ribs.

"But why, *patrón*?"

"Open the door!"

"But I'm already in bed, *patrón*."

Then she heard him going away down the long verandas, stamping his feet the way he always did when he was angry.

The next night, to avoid annoying him again, she left the door half open and got into bed naked, so that he wouldn't have the least difficulty.

But Pedro Páramo never came back.

Even now, when she was the head of all the servants at the Media Luna, when she was old and respected, she still thought of that night the *patrón* said: "Damiana, open the door!"

She went back to bed, thinking how happy Margarita must be at that moment.

A while later she heard a knocking again, but this time at the great gate. It was as if they were pounding at it with gun butts.

She got up and looked out once more. She couldn't see anything, but it seemed to her the ground was boiling the way it does when it rains and the worms come out. She thought she could sense the heat and smell of a whole crowd of men. She heard the croaking of the frogs. The crickets. The night sounds of the rainy season. Then the gun butts hammering at the door again.

A lamp shone on the faces of a group of men, and went out.

"It's nothing that concerns me," Damiana Cisneros said as she closed the window.

"They told me you were defeated, Damasio. Why did you let it happen?"

"They didn't tell you the truth, *patrón*. Nothing's happened to me. I've got seven hundred men here with me, and a few others nearby. What happened was that some of the 'veterans' like that Perseverancio got tired of doing nothing, so they fired on a patrol. It turned out to be a whole army. Villa's troops, you know."

"Where are they from?"

"From the north. They wreck everything they find. They're so strong I don't think anybody can beat them."

"Why don't you join up with them, then? I've already told you to join whoever's winning."

"I already have."

"Then why did you come here to see me?"

"We need money, *patrón*. We're sick of eating meat, sick and tired of it. And nobody'll give us credit. We came here to tell you because we don't want to start robbing anybody. If we weren't keeping so near it wouldn't make any difference, but we're all from this valley and we don't want to rob our own people. So we need some money, even if it's just to buy a little chile. We're fed up with eating meat."

"I'm glad you take care of your men, Damasio, but there're other ways of getting what you need. If you can't get by with what I gave you, why don't you attack Contla? What are you in the revolution for anyway? If you have to come begging you're defeated already. You'd do better to go back to your wife and tend the chickens. Go raid some village! If you're going to risk your hide, why the devil shouldn't other people help out? Contla's full of rich men. Take a little away from them. Or maybe they think you're their wet nurse and have to take care of them? No, Damasio. Make them see this isn't just a game.

You'll get all the money you need."

"Whatever you say, *patrón*. You always give me good advice."

"Then I hope it does you some good."

Pedro Páramo watched the men going away. He heard the hoofbeats of their horses as they disappeared into the night, and smelled the sweat and dust, and felt the trembling of the earth. When he saw the fireflies shining again he realized that all the men had gone. He was alone, like a tree trunk beginning to rot away inside.

He thought of Susana San Juan, then of the girl he had slept with a short while ago. That startled, trembling little body. Her heart in her mouth from fear. "A handful of flesh," he called her. And when he embraced her he tried to change her body into that of Susana San Juan. "A woman who isn't of this world."

At daybreak the day gives a turn, slowly. You can almost hear the rusty hinges of the world. The vibration of this ancient world as it tilts the darkness off itself.

"Is it true that the night is full of sins, Justina?"

"Yes, Susana."

"And is it true?"

"It has to be, Susana."

"And what do you think life is, Justina, except a sin? Don't you hear? Don't you hear the way the world is creaking? Listen!"

"No, Susana, I don't hear a thing. I'm not as fortunate as you are."

"You'd be astonished. You'd be astonished if you could hear the things I can."

Justina went on straightening up the room. She ran the mop over the wet floor. Mopped up the water from the broken vase. Picked up the flowers. Put the broken glass into the pail.

"How many birds have you killed in your life, Justina?"

"A lot of them, Susana."

"And haven't you felt sorry?"

"Yes, Susana."

"Then why are you still waiting to die?"

"I'm waiting for death to come for me, Susana."

"If that's all, it'll come. Don't be worried."

Susana San Juan was propped up against the pillows. Her eyes were restless, glancing everywhere, and her hands were clasped on her stomach like a protecting shell. There were light, humming noises flitting like wings above her head. And the sound of the pulley at the well. And the sounds people make as they wake up.

"Do you believe in Hell, Justina?"

"Yes, Susana. And in Heaven, too."

"I just believe in Hell."

She closed her eyes.

When Justina left the room, Susana San Juan was asleep again and the sun was shining. She met Pedro Páramo outside.

"How is she?"

She shook her head.

"What does she complain about?"

"Nothing, señor. That's just the trouble. You know what they say, that the dead never complain."

"Has Father Rentería come to see her?"

"He came last night to hear confession. She should have received Communion this morning, but I don't think she's in His grace, because Father Rentería hasn't come back. He said he'd be here the first thing, but you can see where the sun is and he still hasn't come. I'm afraid she isn't in His grace."

"Whose grace?"

"God's, señor."

"Don't be a ninny, Justina."

"Just as you say, señor."

Pedro Páramo opened the door and went over to her, letting a ray of light fall across her face. He saw that her eyes were shut tight, as if she felt some inward pain. That her mouth was damp and half open. And then her blind hands, plucking at the sheet, revealed her naked body. It began to thrash with convulsions.

He reached across the bed and covered her up. Her body still twisted and writhed like a wounded snake, each spasm more violent than the last. He put his lips to her ear and spoke to her: "Susana!"

Again: "Susana!"

The door opened and Father Rentería came in. "I'm going to give you Communion, my child."

He stood waiting while Pedro Páramo raised her up against the pillows and the headboard.

Susana San Juan, between sleeping and waking, extended her tongue and swallowed the Host. Then she said: "We've had a lovely time today, Florencio." And she buried herself again in the tomb of her bedclothes.

"Do you see that window there, Doña Fausta, out in the Media Luna? The one where the light's always burning?"

"No, Angeles, I can't see any window."

"That's because it just went dark. Do you think something bad has happened in the Media Luna? That window's been lit for over three years now, night after night. I talked with somebody who's been out there and she said it's the bedroom of Pedro Páramo's wife. The poor thing's out of her mind and she's afraid of the dark . . . and look, there isn't any light. Isn't that a bad sign?"

"Maybe she's dead. I heard she was very sick. They even say she didn't recognize anybody, and was always talking to herself. Just think how Don Pedro punished himself by marrying her!"

"I know. Poor Don Pedro."

"No, Fausta. He deserves it. And a lot more besides."

"Look, the window's still dark."

"Forget the window. It's awfully late for a couple of old crones to be roaming the streets. We'd better go home."

And the two women, who had left the church at about eleven, disappeared into the shadows of the arcade. They saw the figure of a man crossing the plaza in the direction of the Media Luna.

"Look, Doña Fausta, doesn't that look like Doctor Valencia?"

"Yes, it does. Though I'm so nearsighted I really can't make him out."

"Remember that he always wears a black coat and white trousers. I'll bet you something bad has happened in the Media Luna, or he wouldn't be walking that fast."

"You're right, it must be something serious. I'd like to go back and tell Father Rentería that he ought to go out there, so the poor thing won't die without confessing."

"Don't worry, Angeles, God wouldn't let it happen. After all she's suffered in this world, He wouldn't let her die without spiritual help and go on suffering in the next. Although the mystics say that crazy people don't need to confess, that they're innocent even if their souls aren't clean. Well, only God knows about that. . . . Look, there's a light in the window again! I hope everything turns out all right. We've just got the church all decorated for Christmas, and you can imagine what would happen to all our work if somebody should die in that house. With the power Don Pedro has, he'd ruin everything in a minute."

"You're always looking for the worst, Doña Fausta. You should do what I do and leave everything to Divine Providence. Say an Ave Maria and I'm sure nothing bad will happen between now and tomorrow morning."

"Believe me, Angeles, you always know how to make me feel better. I'm going to go to sleep with your thoughts in my mind. They say the thoughts you think when you're asleep go straight up to Heaven. I just hope mine can reach that far. Good night."

"Good night, Fausta."

The two old women went into their houses. The silence of the night closed down again over the village.

"My mouth is filled with dirt."

"Yes, Father."

"Don't say, 'Yes, Father.' Just repeat what I tell you."

"But what are you going to tell me? Why do I have to confess all over again?"

"This isn't confession, Susana. I've only come to talk with you. To prepare you for death."

"Am I going to die?"

"Yes, child."

"Then why don't you leave me alone? I want to rest. They must have brought you here to keep me awake. To drive away my sleep. And how will I find it again? I won't, Father. Please let me rest."

"I will, Susana. If you'll just repeat what I say, you can go back to sleep. It'll be like crooning to yourself, and once you're asleep again, nobody will wake you up. Ever."

"All right, Father. I'll do what you say."

Father Rentería was sitting on the edge of the bed. He put his hands on her shoulders and brought his mouth next to her ear, to whisper his words in secret: "My mouth is filled with dirt." Then he stopped. He tried to see if her lips were moving. They moved, but no sound came out of them.

"My mouth is filled with yours, with your kisses. Your hard lips biting and crushing mine . . ."

She glanced sideways at Father Rentería, but she could only see him dimly, as if he were behind a clouded window. Then she heard his voice again in her ear:

"I swallow the froth of my saliva. I eat clods of earth. They are crawling with worms. They choke my throat and rasp against my palate. . . . My lips loosen, grimacing, and my teeth rend and devour them. My face dissolves, my eyes melt to slime, my hair goes up in flames . . ."

He wondered at her stillness. He would have liked to divine her thoughts, to watch her heart struggle to resist the images he was sowing within her. He looked into her eyes, and she returned his look. He thought he could see her lips forming in a smile.

"There is still more. The vision of God. The gentle light of His infinite Heaven. The joy of the cherubim and the songs of the seraphim. The happiness in God's eyes, the last, fleeting vision of those who are condemned to eternal suffering. Earthly suffering is as nothing to those torments. The marrow of our bones is turned to fire, and our veins to threads of flame. And the terrible agony never lessens: it is kindled forever by God's wrath."

"He held me in his arms. He loved me."

Father Rentería looked at the figures that stood around him, waiting for the final moment. Pedro Páramo was standing near the door with his arms crossed. Next to him, Doctor Valencia. Then several other men. Farther away, in the shadows, a handful of women, the kind who can hardly wait to start praying for the deceased.

He intended to get up. To give her extreme unction and say: "I have finished." But no, he still hadn't finished. He couldn't administer the sacraments without being sure she had repented.

He began to have doubts. Perhaps there wasn't anything for her to repent. Perhaps there wasn't anything for him to pardon. He leaned over her again and gently shook her by the shoulders. "You are going into God's presence," he said in a low voice. "And His judgment against sinners is harsh."

Then he put his lips to her ear once more, but she shook her head: "Go away, Father! Don't worry about me. I feel calm now and I want to go to sleep."

A woman hidden in the shadows began to sob.

Susana San Juan seemed to regain life. She sat up in bed to say: "Justina, will you please do your crying somewhere else!"

Then she felt that her head was crushing into her stomach.

She tried to separate them, to push her stomach aside, it was blinding her eyes and cutting off her breath, but her head pressed down and down, as if it were sinking into the darkness of the night.

"I was there. I saw Doña Susana die."

"What did you say, Dorotea?"

"What I just got through saying."

At daybreak the village was awakened by the ringing of the bells. It was the morning of the eighth of December. A gray morning, but not cold. The ringing began with the largest bell, and the others followed it. A few people thought they were ringing for High Mass, and began to open their doors. But only a few, only those who wake up before dawn and lie awake until the first bells tell them the night has ended. But the ringing went on longer than it should have. And it was not only the bells of the main church, but also those of the Sangre de Cristo, the Cruz Verde, even the Santuario. At noon they were still ringing, and at nightfall. They rang day and night, day and night, louder and louder and louder. The people of the village had to shout in order to hear what they were saying. "What's happened?" they asked.

After three days everybody was deaf. It was impossible to talk with that clamor filling the air. And the bells rang and rang, some of them cracked now, with a dead, hollow sound.

"Doña Susana's dead."

"Dead? Who?"

"His wife."

"Whose?"

"Pedro Páramo's."

The endless ringing began to draw people in from other places. They came in from Contla almost as if on a pilgrimage. And from farther away. A circus arrived from somewhere, with a merry-go-round and a ferris wheel. And then the musicians. They were only spectators at first, but soon they were playing in the bandstand in the plaza. Little by little the occasion turned into a fiesta. Comala was so crowded it was difficult to take a step.

The ringing stopped at last, but not the fiesta. There was no way to explain to the crowd that the bells rang for the dead, no way to make them go home. On the contrary, more and more arrived.

The Media Luna was silent. All of the servants walked barefoot and talked in whispers. Susana San Juan was buried in the graveyard, but hardly anybody in Comala even knew about it. Because of the fiesta. The cockfights and the music. The shouts of the vendors and the drunkards. The village was all lights and noise, and the Media Luna was all shadows and silence. Pedro Páramo wouldn't speak, wouldn't leave his room. He swore he'd get revenge on Comala:

"I'll fold my arms and Comala will starve to death."

And that was what he did.

El Tilcuate kept coming back: "We're with Carranza now."

"All right."

"And General Obregón."

"Good."

"But they've made peace. We don't have anything to do."

"Wait. Keep your men armed. That peace won't last very long."

"Father Rentería has taken up arms. Should we be for him or against him?"

"Keep on the government's side."

"But we're irregulars. They treat us like rebels."

"Then go take a rest."

"How can I?"

"Do whatever you want, then."

"I think I'll join the Father's men. I like the way they shout. Besides, he can save our souls if anything happens."

"Do whatever you want."

Pedro Páramo was sitting in an old leather chair by the great gate of the Media Luna. It was a little before the last shadows of the night disappeared. He had been sitting there, alone, for over three hours. He didn't sleep. He had forgotten about sleep, and about time itself: "Old people don't sleep very much. Hardly at all. We may doze a little, sometimes, but we never stop thinking. That's all I've got left to do." Then he added in a loud voice: "It won't be long now. It won't be long."

And he went on: "It's been a long time since you left me, Susana. The light was the same as it is now. Not so reddish, but just as weak and cold, because the sun was hidden by the clouds. Everything's the same. It's even the same moment. I was here at the gate, watching the dawn. Watching you go away. Watching you climb the path to Heaven. And Heaven opened up, and light streamed out. You left the shadows of this world behind you. You vanished into Heaven's light.

"It was the last time I saw you. You passed among the boughs of the paradise trees that stand along the path, and their last leaves drifted behind you. Then you disappeared. I cried, 'Come back, Susana!'"

Pedro Páramo continued to move his lips, to whisper words. Later he closed his mouth and half opened his eyes. They reflected the faint light of daybreak.

At the same hour Doña Inés, the mother of Gamaliel Villalpando, was sweeping the street in front of her son's shop. She had left the door ajar, and Abundio Martínez went inside. He found Gamaliel asleep on the counter, with his sombrero over his face to keep off the flies. He waited for him to wake up. Finally Doña Inés came in from the street and poked her son in the ribs with the handle of the broom.

"You've got a customer!" she said. "Get up!"

Gamaliel grunted and raised himself up on one elbow. His eyes were bloodshot because he had been up half the night waiting on the drunkards and getting drunk along with them. He sat up on the counter, swore at his mother, swore at himself, and swore worst of all at life, that "isn't worth a damn." Then he lay down again, with his hands between his legs, and went back to sleep still muttering curses:

"It's not my fault if the damned drunks are still on the loose."

"My poor son. Excuse him, Abundio. The poor thing spent most of the night with some travelers that were drinking here.

What brings you around so early?"

She shouted her words because Abundio was deaf.

"It's just that I need a pint of alcohol."

"Has Refugio fainted again?"

"She's dead, Mother Villa. She died last night, about eleven. And I even sold my burros. I even sold my burros to get her well."

"I can't hear what you're saying! Or aren't you saying anything? What did you say?"

"That I sat up all night with my wife. With Refugio. She died last night."

"No wonder I could smell death! Imagine, I even said to Gamaliel here: 'I can smell that somebody's died in the village.' But he didn't listen because he was getting drunk along with those travelers. And you know that when he's drinking everything makes him laugh and he doesn't pay attention to anything. But tell me, who have you got for the wake?"

"Nobody. That's why I want the alcohol."

"Straight?"

"Yes, Mother Villa. I can get drunk faster that way. And I'd like it right now, because I'm in a hurry."

"Seeing it's you, you can have it at half price. Be sure to tell your wife that I always was fond of her and that I hope she'll remember me when she's in Heaven."

"All right, Mother Villa."

"And tell her before she starts decaying too much."

"I will. And I know she's counting on you to pray for her. She didn't die in peace, because there wasn't anybody to help her soul."

"What? Didn't you go get Father Rentería?"

"Yes. But they told me he was in the mountains."

"Mountains? What mountains?"

"I didn't ask. It's on account of the revolution."

"Do you mean to say he went too? I pity us, Abundio."

"What does it matter to us? Pour me some more. Look at Gamaliel, Mother Villa, he's sound asleep again."

"But don't you forget to tell Refugio to pray for me in Heaven. I need all the help I can get."

"Don't worry. I'll tell her as soon as I get back. I'll even make her give me her promise."

"That's right, that's just the thing to do. Because you know the way women are, you always have to keep after them."

Abundio Martínez tossed another twenty centavos onto the counter.

"Give me the rest of it, Mother Villa. And if you want to give me more than I've paid for, that's up to you. I'm going to drink it with Refugio. With my Cuca."

"Go ahead, then, Abundio, before Gamaliel wakes up. He always has an awful temper after he's been drinking. And don't forget to tell your wife what I said."

He was sneezing as he left the shop, because that alcohol was pure fire. But they said you could get drunk faster if you drank it straight. He'd drunk it straight. Fanning his mouth with his shirttails.

He meant to go straight home. Refugio was waiting for him. But he turned in the wrong direction and started walking down the street that led out of the village.

"Damiana!" Pedro Páramo called. "Somebody's coming. Find out what he wants."

Abundio staggered down the road, sometimes on his feet,

sometimes on all fours. The ground was rocking. Spinning. Sliding out from under him. He grabbed it with both hands, but it got away again. He saw a man sitting in a chair near a doorway. He stopped.

"Give me a little money. Just a little. I have to bury my wife."

Damiana Cisneros was praying. "Save us, Lord. Save us from evil." She made the sign of the cross.

Abundio Martínez saw a woman. She looked frightened. She was making the sign of the cross in front of him. He trembled and looked behind him. There wasn't any demon there. There wasn't anybody at all.

"Please," he said. "I have to bury my wife."

The sun was over his shoulder. It had come out only a few minutes before. It was blurred by a cloud of dust.

Pedro Páramo covered his face with his hands, as if he were hiding from the light. The screams of Damiana Cisneros raced out over the fields: "They're killing Don Pedro!"

Abundio Martínez could hear that the woman was screaming. He tried to think of some way to stop her, but he couldn't make his thoughts work right. He knew her screams could be heard a long way off. Perhaps even his wife could hear them, because they were so loud they pierced his ears, although he couldn't understand the words. He thought of his wife back there, all alone, stretched out on her cot in the patio of his house. He had put her out there so the night air would cool her and she wouldn't start smelling so soon. Cuca, who had gone to bed with him the night before, still alive, still romping like a filly, biting him and rubbing her nose against his. Cuca, who gave him that little son that died as soon as it was born, because of her ailments they said, her chills and fevers and eyesores and all the other things she suffered from, as he told the doctor when he went to get him at the last moment, and had to sell his burros because he charged so much. . . . Cuca, back there in the dew now, with her eyes closed. Without being able to see the daybreak. This one or any other.

"Help me!" he said. "Give me a little money!"

But he couldn't hear himself speak. That woman's screams had left him deaf.

Black dots were moving along the Comala road. Soon they changed into men, and then they were almost here. Damiana Cisneros stopped screaming. She stopped making the sign of the cross. She fell. Her mouth was open, as if she were yawning.

The men lifted her up off the ground and carried her into the house.

"Are you all right, *patrón*?" they asked.

Pedro Páramo only nodded his head.

They disarmed Abundio, who still held the bloody knife in his hand.

"Come along," they said. "You've really got yourself in trouble."

And he followed them.

Just before they reached Comala he asked permission. He went to one side and began vomiting. It was a bilious yellow. Streams and streams of it, as if he had drunk gallons of water. Then his head began to throb, and his tongue felt thick.

"I'm drunk," he said.

He went back to where they were waiting. He leaned on their shoulders and they dragged him along. His feet scratched a long furrow in the dirt.

Pedro Páramo was still sitting in his leather chair, watching them go toward the village. When he tried to raise his left hand he felt it fall dead on his knees, but he didn't pay any attention to it. He was used to seeing some part of himself die each day. He could see the paradise trees swaying as they dropped their leaves. "Everybody chooses the same path. Everybody goes away." Then he went back to the place where he had left his thoughts.

"Susana," he said, and closed his eyes. "I begged you to come back . . .

". . . There was a full moon overhead. I couldn't stop looking at you. The moonlight bathed your face. I looked and looked at the vision that you were. Soft and shining in the moonlight. Your lips moist and shining with stars. Your body turning transparent in the dew. Susana. Susana San Juan."

He tried to raise his hand to make the image clearer, but it lay on his knees as if it were stone. He tried to raise his other hand, but it fell at his side, slowly, until it rested on the ground, like a crutch holding up his useless shoulder.

"I am dying," he said.

The sun revolved above the earth, bringing back forms and shapes. His ruined lands stretched out in front of him, empty. The heat warmed his body. His eyes hardly moved. They were leaping from memory to memory, erasing the present. Suddenly his heart paused, and it seemed as if time paused also. And the breath of life.

"So that there won't be another night," he thought.

Because he was afraid of the nights. Of the phantoms that surrounded him in the darkness.

"I know Abundio will be back here in a little while with his bloody hands, to keep begging for the help I wouldn't give him. And I can't lift up my hands to cover my eyes and not see him. I'll have to listen to him until his voice fades away with the daylight. Until his voice dies out."

He felt a pair of hands touching his shoulders and he straightened up.

"Don Pedro," Damiana said, "don't you want me to bring you your dinner?"

Pedro Páramo said, "No. I'll go in."

He leaned against Damiana and tried to walk. After a few steps he fell down, pleading within but not speaking a single word. He struck a feeble blow against the ground and then crumbled to pieces as if he were a heap of stones.